For Melissa, I wouldn't have done this without your help.

DEMON
CROSSING

CRYSTAL
CASTLE

QUADRANT

Cardia

UNLIKELY QUEEN

The prophecy foretold of the true queen...

In the new world, where the old world is long forgotten, an evil queen sits on the throne, and anyone who challenges her reign is a mortal enemy—I am that enemy just by breathing.

The queen always gets what she wants, and she wants me dead.

Then one day, my life is turned upside down by a prophecy naming me the one true queen. I was oblivious to the true roles of the two men in my life—the Angel of Light and the Angel of Death—as my existence hung in the balance. One man there to save me, the other to claim me should the queen succeed in her quest for my blood.

But every time she nearly succeeds in my demise, my dark angel swoops in, pulling me back to safety. Making the world stop. Pulling everything back in balance.

Tired of being hunted by the vampires, slaves to the queen, I decide to fight back. It's the only way to survive. I'm going to tear down the wards one by one and free my allies—the witches and the wolves—and then I'm going to force the queen from the safety of her castle and claim what's rightfully mine.

Her kingdom.

Her throne.

Her crown.

Chapter One

His touch brands my very soul. I can feel it all the way down to the depths of my bones. It's like a fire licking at its victim and being drenched in ice water at the same time. His lips touch mine, branding me, marking my soul so anyone and everyone can see or feel it.

I am his.

In this moment and forever, I belong to him.

It feels like I'm in a daze. I shouldn't know what he's doing, but somehow, I know every single detail. It's like a puzzle in my head, working it out, putting it together piece by piece.

A sweep of his tongue, and the fire smolders.

A bite of my lip, and the fire burns brighter.

My insides are shaking, not understanding but

wanting as much as he can give to quench my insatiable need for him.

He pulls back, and in an instant, everything changes. I'm not blind. I can see clearly. His eyes shine brightly into mine, silver and steady. It feels like a drug is clearing from my system, cleansing me of him. I crave his intoxication once more—a hit—that one single touch or a single look can give.

"You feel it, don't you?" My eyes close at the sound of his voice, and I shiver as it takes on an edge. "Now I need you to run... run as if your life depends on it. Because if you don't, I will find you, and I will take you."

Is it a malicious promise or a delicious threat? What I do know is that it's one I delight in.

"The prophecy?" I ask, and he nods in answer, wings expanding out in all their glory.

And I find myself craving him once more.

"If it comes true..." he continues by way of warning, "...our worlds will intertwine. You will have more power than anyone could ever dream of, and no one will be able to stop you."

"You won't touch me again?"

I miss it already—his touch, his taste.

"I won't be able to." His lips meet my cheek, then the same words whisper once more in my ear. "Run, little fighter. Run."

Chapter Two

All I want is to sleep right now, but Tanya is pushing my leg, trying to wake me. Kicking her, she falls backward, and I hear her hit the floor in a heap as I smile under the sheets.

"You bitch," she hisses.

I pull the covers down as she rights herself at the end of the bed. She looks gorgeous, dressed and ready for whatever today will bring. With her hands on her hips, Tanya throws me her most menacing death stare, which is nowhere near as severe as she thinks. She wants to cuss me out—I can see it on her face—but she won't. Tatiana is near, and she hates cuss words, unless they're from her own mouth, that is.

I am the baby of my family. Tatiana is the eldest, with Tanya being the middle child. There are exactly three years between each of our births, with the three of us sharing a birthday. We also share the same thick, chocolate-brown hair and emerald-green eyes.

They say we look like our mother, who we miss deeply. It's been years since she died. When you get sick in Cardia, only the rich get the help they need. Every potion we concocted to heal her, every mixture of herbs we tried to make her pain more tolerable, never worked on her.

And in the end, the sickness took her.

The word they used to define it was cancer. Today, it's sickness.

We have never met any other family like ours, but there aren't many families left in Cardia. Cardia was established before I was born and after things had changed for the worse. Our kind never mixed with others before the angels descended, taking over a world we are all deemed too incompetent to manage.

When they arrived, angry and condemning our actions, they destroyed everything we knew to be home and relocated us to what we now know as Cardia. Not everyone cooperated with the forced transition, many arguing that the angels had no right to exercise their authority in such a manner. While some never got to see Cardia for themselves, others—including my family —were lumped into their own wards.

That means we now have to play nice in the event we cross paths with ones considered undesirables.

Those who survived are different and rarely ever see eye to eye. A mere grudge that had festered for thousands of years, beginning in the Biblical age, still haunts us in our present life.

My family are descendants of the great Witch of Endor, who had once been sought out by King Saul. Saul was a fierce, competitive man hell-bent on being anointed a prophet, his desire blinding him to a troublesome future that awaited. One particular night, under the glow of the new moon on the hill of Gibeah, he chanted his spell—a spell the Witch of Endor guaranteed would see his anointment.

It worked.

Until it became a curse.

On the battlefield fighting against the Philistines, King Saul fell on his sword, taking his own life.

When all had fallen quiet, death surrounding him, and with the new moon exactly four years on the leap year later, King Saul rose from his sword.

He wasn't himself.

No longer the ruler of Gibeah.

No longer living.

His tongue flicked over the sharpened points of his eye teeth, the thirst for blood sending him into a rabid frenzy of both disgust and need.

He didn't know the monster he'd become.

This was never meant to happen.

Before he could feast, there was one thing he needed to do first—kill the Witch of Endor.

That night, as the few surviving books tell us, King Saul—who was now a vampire—sought out the Witch of Endor and took her blood while she slept. He feasted on her with an insatiable thirst. He found her taste addictive, the witch's potent blood coursing through his veins, making him feel more alive than ever. By the time Saul made to leave, the empty vessel of the deceitful woman beneath him, he had vowed he would destroy every living witch on earth.

King Saul was then on a warpath, ending human lives until the sun disappeared behind the mountains. Like him, they rose from the dead with no pulse, no heartbeat, sharpened teeth, a paler skin than their surviving Arabian family, and an unrelenting craving for blood. Many lost their lives, and the only ones who noticed the stealth-like figure in the night were the werewolves. They watched from afar, their yellow eyes tracking the movements of a murderous man who'd taken the life of their ally—the Witch of Endor.

For years, the wolves and vampires battled each other.

The wolves were advocates of peace.

The pales, as the wolves referred to them, only cared about one thing—building their army. Eventually, their army was so great, the vampires forced the wolves into slavery, which lasted for centuries.

Fast forward to today, and the resentment and hostility between the two clans is still raw.

Then we have the humans. There aren't many of them left, but the ones who did survive the angel fallout live a lowly existence. A life dependent on the vampires. In order to stay alive, the humans offer a percentage of their blood to feed the vampires. Each token grants them an extra month on earth. This isn't a gift given for a chance at their own survival, it's purely because if the vamps suck their bodies clean, they would soon run short of humans to feast on.

No humans equal vampire death.

No humans mean that we, the witches, will become the next target.

Then lastly, we have the angels. Strong, beautifully fierce creatures who can rage with the wrath of God one moment and nurture the weak the next. They are rulers of their realm and rulers of shifters and witches on Earth. The angels created and enforced the law of the land, which happened when I was only a child, just eleven years old. I can't remember the time before them, but the glimpses of what my sisters say make it sound beautiful.

The males, like most creatures on Earth, are more magnificent than their female counterparts. Their strong, angular jaws speak of power and a presence that can both fascinate and intimidate. They are fiercely built, capable of winning any war, not only with their muscled strength but their agile minds. We, my family of witches and I, haven't had much to do with them, keen to avoid their scrutiny.

Until today.

Today, everything changed.

Today, we felt the wrath of the angels.

It wasn't a day I expected to come, it wasn't a strange day, or anything out of the ordinary. Our routine was the same. Every morning, Tatiana heads our training, pushing us to our limits. It is essential training in order to survive living so close to volatile wards of shifters and vamps.

"You know Tatiana will be pissed if you aren't dressed in ten. So, hurry up," Tanya warns, storming out of my room.

More reluctant than usual, I crawl out of bed and dress in casual black clothes—what everyone seems to wear. Wearing color outside your ward makes you stand out, which is something to be avoided at all costs.

Our house is small, boarded, and plain in a deliberate effort to avert attention from the outside world. It has three bedrooms, one for each of us, and a communal living area where we eat our meals.

We don't own any of the electronics I read about in my books. They are a thing of the past and something I never had a chance to experience. Instead, I read novels by authors long since passed, about mythical worlds and once-famous people.

Training is grueling but necessary. Tatiana teaches us what she has learned from books I found at the library and from what our mother taught her. She can't read, so the pictures are interpreted as best as possible.

We quickly find out if the moves are effective or not, and this morning is no exception. In a swift Kung Fu motion, Tatiana flips Tanya on her back, leaving her wheezing for breath. I wince, almost feeling the pain myself.

Tatiana spots me in the doorway, and in a heartbeat, issues my chores for the day. "Talia, you need to go to the markets and get bread. Tanya, go to the castle headquarters and pay our way."

We don't argue, we never do. She seems to know all but in a good way. She has kept us alive and protected us for as long I can remember, and we respect her position in the family. She hands me some currency, enough red tokens to buy the basics. We are far from wealthy. We rarely ever possess orange tokens, which could be splurged by stocking our cupboards for days, and we certainly never hold any green tokens in our hands, which would identify us as the wealthy elite.

Kissing my sisters on the cheek, Tatiana stops me with a hand on my shoulder. "Straight there, straight home." Her eyes shine bright like they always do when she worries. She has every right to be concerned. Tensions are high over a mysterious vanishing of a teenage witch. No one has seen her. No one has heard from her. It's a mystery that has rattled the ward and has us all on edge. We never know if we are fully safe despite the angels' rule.

"Here," she declares, handing me a small, black bag containing weapons. It's against the Cardia law to carry weapons, and I'd face serious consequences if I am caught, but I don't have a choice.

"I'll be fine. I'll see you soon." I smile reassuringly while buttoning my black coat.

I set out on foot and navigate through our ward. The market's set in the middle, in a quadrant framed by the wards. If you don't possess the power to fly, you walk. Although witches certainly have the power, it's a mutual understanding that we remain low-key, thus blending in with the others. Hostilities are rife, and Tatiana's adamant we never draw attention to ourselves.

When I enter the quadrant, it's super busy with shoppers. And when I spot the line of those wanting to buy bread, I decide to look around until it ebbs. Three stalls along, I see a hat, colorful in bright pink. I'm drawn immediately and pick it from the rack to study it closer. Instantly, I tense, my personal space being invaded. Then I hear a noise.

Someone is smelling me, inhaling deeply as they travel the length of my neck. Unsettling chills break out along my skin, and I turn, lifting my shoulder for protection, only to see the vampire recoil. This isn't the first time it has happened in my life. For some unforetold reason, vampires are both repulsed and uniquely curious over my scent.

He snatches the hat from my hands, looking at me with a snarl. "You can't afford that."

"I'm only looking," I defend myself.

"You're a witch, aren't you?" He squints as if assessing me. "You're not like your sisters."

I ignore him.

The vamps have us all picked. In the event the humans revolt, the bloodsuckers will turn to us. As a result of this impending doom, they have practically marked us for their taking, knowing our scents and picking their favorites.

"Excuse me." I make to leave, but he blocks me. Instead of meeting his red irises, I look at his shoulder with my jaw clenched.

The vampire inhales me again, deeply, drawing me

in until finally he exhales. With a deep voice he rumbles, "What are you?"

At that point, I'm left with little choice. I push past his cold, hard body and stumble back onto the path. I can feel his eyes burning into me as I quickly sink into a crowd of people, willing myself to blend in again with the masses.

When I come to a stop in the bread line, I'm trembling. The encounter was like so many I've had before, each one leaving me more on edge and uneasy for what's to come.

I distract myself by watching others. In front of me is a large man, both tall and wide. He is all mass with a thick head of hair, and his impatience is evident with the continual cracking of his knuckles. In front of him is one of the witches who lives a few blocks away. She is wealthy and doesn't hide it well. She stands clutching her bag tightly to her chest as if she fears being robbed.

My shoulders finally relax some, then I'm suddenly jolted forward with a haphazard push in the back. I lose my footing and fall against the tall, burly man's back. He is quick to turn his bright yellow eyes behind him, scolding me. *A werewolf.* He glances at whoever is behind me and his yellow eyes fade back to brown in an instant. The hairs on my neck stand on end, and I'm suddenly terrified to turn around. Whoever it is that can rattle the shifter is no friend of mine.

Instead, my shoulders grow tense once again, and I swallow hard. This is why Tatiana gives me a bag of weapons every time I leave the house. I want to walk away, but I'm frozen. I want to breathe, but my lungs are locked tight.

And then...

...I feel him.

His hard chest presses against my small back, and I shiver. It's not the cold body of the vamp, though, it's someone else. I can feel his heartbeat. I can hear him breathe me in just like the vamp did, his breath setting my neck to tingling.

I want to run, away from him. How can he set this off in me? And who is he? I don't think I actually want to know who it is. Because anyone who wants to invade my space this way isn't someone I would want to know. Managing to take a shaky breath, I try to calm myself. I can still feel him at the base of my neck.

He doesn't say a word.

He doesn't move.

When I take a step forward, he does too, until we are once again touching. We continue this until I get to the counter. The mistress baker looks at me with a smile that quickly fades when she sees who is behind me.

My hand is shaking when I hand her the token, and she avoids all eye contact. Only when I accept the bread and move to the side to exit the line do I see who it is.

An angel.

One I have seen before many times but only from afar.

His masculine beauty is something I always admire. The angel is dressed all in white, his hair pushed back and silver eyes locked on me. His white trench coat almost hits the ground, and he carries the air of authority all angels possess. He looks out of place here where everyone wears black. All angels are beautiful, handsome, but this one holds something else that makes you wet your lips with your tongue.

Those around us mirror the mistress baker, their gazes downcast as they scurry in different directions. But I can't move. I'm caught in his eyes, left staring at their magnificence. They shine bright, like pure silver radiating from the irises. In turn, he studies me. The angel cocks his head slightly to the side, eyes traveling the length of my body. I swallow hard at the attention and am unsure how to deal with it. The corners of his lips twitch, and something inside me stirs.

He creates more questions than answers, and that alone makes me step back. Breaking his hypnotic hold on me, I take off in the direction I came, my hands shaking and my breathing laboured, not allowing myself to glance behind me on my way.

Just like the vampire, I can feel the angel watching me, his impenetrable gaze burning into me as I make my escape.

But unlike the vampire's culinary desires, the angel comes with a much more sinister warning. Trouble is brewing, and I have no idea what it is or how to stop it.

Chapter Three

I find Tatiana in the kitchen preparing dinner as I walk inside. When her knife stills and she looks up to see me standing in the doorway, she's immediately confused.

Tanya isn't home yet. She should have been already. When she goes to the castle, she is always at home before I return.

"Did you see Tanya in your travels?" She tries to hide her panic, but I know better.

I shake my head. "She always takes the Eastside because she misses the market crowd."

She slams the knife down on the counter and curses. I know things are bad when she swears. In a heartbeat, Tatiana is past me, running to the door. She swings it open so hard it smashes into the wall, but she is forced to come to a halt. In the doorway, silhouetted by the evening sun, is a figure so large, even I take a step back.

"You need to come with us," a dark and heavy voice commands.

I don't move, and I wait for Tatiana to give some instruction.

"Why?" she asks, mustering authority.

"We don't answer to you," he replies, cool and calm, yet the tone is loaded with a warning. Angels have been known to not answer to no one, so why do they answer to her?

Tatiana's hand grips the door, knuckles white as she turns to me. "Stay here and wait for Tanya."

I nod, unable to speak. I count five angels on the porch. To have one angel pay you a visit is intimidating enough, but to have five is downright terrifying and unheard of.

"You are both required." The angel stops Tatiana and looks over her shoulder at me. "Immediately."

Tatiana shakes her head. "No, she stays here! I will come and sort out whatever it is you need." She's always in protective mode. Always.

"It is not negotiable, witch. Come of your own accord, or force will be used."

Tatiana turns on her heel, eyes flashing with urgency. At the same time, the heavy-handed angel pushes past her, dominating the room. There is no point in using magic. It's five against two, their strength much more powerful than ours.

"Run! Run, Talia!" she yells, and I do what she says. It's what she has always told me to do if ever we are faced with this situation. My feet move fast and I flee past our bedrooms, through the kitchen, and out the back door. I jump from the top of the four steps to the grass and turn left toward the neighbor's house. Our neighbor, Francis, who was our mother's good friend, a reclusive witch, is probably watching all the commotion from her windows but will offer little assistance. In this instance... no one will help us. Her yard backs up to a narrow path that will lead me to the main road. I need to get to the wolves' ward. There, they will demand to know what's going on. Why three sister witches are suddenly being targeted. They are our allies.

But I'll never make it.

I come to a skidding halt, falling backward on my heels until I hit the ground. There, appearing before me, stands the angel from the market. In his beautifully frightening presence, he holds me captive. I'm going nowhere. His eyes, just like they had earlier on, shine brightly with intensity, his gaze penetrating mine.

"Why are you running?" he asks, confused at the

thought I would run. Angels aren't used to people not obeying their every command.

"Why are you chasing us?"

"We require you and your sisters back at the Crystal Castle."

"But we haven't done anything wrong."

"It was you I saw at the market today, was it not?"

I frown. He knows quite well it was me, so why is he playing coy? "Yes," I bite back, and he smiles at my irritation.

"Get off the ground," he orders, extending his hand.

It's a kind gesture, but I don't want him close enough to smell or even to touch me.

But what I want doesn't seem to matter. I start righting myself without his help, when he grabs hold of my elbow and pulls me up. He isn't gentle, and a newfound fear pulses through me. Sensing the worst, I push hard against his chest, which feels like a solid boulder beneath my palms. He breaks his grip and his back connects with the tree behind him, snapping off the bark, which falls at his feet. He staggers, trying to balance himself with one hand.

A deep frown mars his handsome face as he studies me. No witch has ever possessed the strength to move an angel even an inch. They are the Alpha and Omega of this universe, and now he knows that the witch he is looking at is not just a witch.

"What are you?" he asks in a coarse whisper. The angel looks behind me, ensuring we are alone.

"I'm a descendant of the Witch of Endor." I'm stating something he already knows. All witches are descendants of the Witch of Endor.

"Where is it you find your strength?"

"Morning practice. My sister trains us well," I half lie. Tatiana is a good trainer, but she goes easy on me because I am stronger than the two of them combined.

"No amount of practice could make any witch that strong."

I remain silent, not giving him what he wants.

Again, his eyes travel the length of my body, but this time, I suspect it's for a different reason. I'm wearing black leather pants combined with a black shirt, my hair tied back. It's what we all wear.

He can't figure me out.

But he wants to.

"The others won't hesitate to put you in line, and believe me, that's something you don't want. You may have caught me unaware of your strength, but you cannot expect to fight them and win. You and your sisters are needed at the Crystal Castle."

"Where is my sister, Tanya?" I ask him without moving to his request.

"At the Crystal Castle."

"Did she do something wrong? Is that why you're holding her there?"

"Move," he orders, breaking eye contact and once again gripping my elbow. "The others are waiting."

I dig my heels in, and he turns on me, silver irises flashing a warning. A few beats pass in a silent standoff.

"Why do you stare?" he challenges.

My eyes narrow to mirror his. "You don't scare me."

"It certainly looked that way back at the market."

"You caught me unaware."

His lips twitch and my gaze is drawn to them.

"Move if you want any answers."

His fingers dig into the flesh of my upper arm, and I wince as he pulls me along at his side. Instead of going back through the house, we cut down along its side until we see the others waiting out front, standing in the dirt, which makes the angels seem out of place in this area.

Tatiana is surrounded by angels, her hands tied behind her back. She, too, must have put up some form of fight, and this is the consequence. They all turn and watch us approach, the defeated look on my sister's face concerning. She is in the dark just like me, having no idea why our family is being targeted, only that we were separated, and that is never a good thing.

Our magic is stronger when we are together. A secret we *never* share with outsiders.

"What took so long, Bronik?" the one who stands behind my sister asks impatiently.

"We're ready now," the one I now know as Bronik responds, dismissing the question. He then looks from me to my sister before asking, "Do I need to restrain you like her?"

"No, but I want to walk with my sister." I move to leave his side, but his hand juts out to take mine, pulling me back to him. There is a zap on contact, leaving his left arm trembling in the aftershock. Again, just like earlier, he frowns, confused over the reaction my body gives to his. When the angel's eyes flick from me to the group and back again, cautious whether they had seen anything, he simply nods and lets me go.

Why he is protecting me? I don't know.

Why he feels the need to keep quiet about something he knows isn't right has me questioning whether he truly is one of the angels I need to fear. When in reality, they all need to be feared.

Joining Tatiana, I meet her scolding gaze. "I told you to run," she seethes quietly, determined to have none of the angels overhear.

"I did! He appeared out of nowhere."

She looks at Bronik with curiosity. "Did you hurt him?"

"Not as much as I wanted to."

"He looks a little miffed. What did you say?"

"Nothing! I pushed him. Hard. He wants to know why I'm so strong."

I hear her swallow. I understand her fear. The angels have never had a rival who could match their strength before. If I am found out, I'm as good as dead.

Navigating through the ward, five glorious angels and two witches, one of them restrained, is causing quite the stir. Neighbors are watching from their porches as we make our procession through the streets. As soon as we hit the quadrant, everyone will be talking. I only hope the werewolf shifters come to our rescue.

Chapter Four

Their heavy footsteps crunch noisily on the ground as they march us through the ward. We walk along the border shared with the werewolves, and I pray they see what is happening to us and intervene. It's still early enough that the border wards are down for shopping. They are our only hope, but something tells me this is a war we will have to fight on our own.

Under her breath, Tatiana whispers a protection spell. It will only do us well for the journey, as once we reach the castle, the spell will simply dissolve into thin air.

"Stop it," I snap a little too harshly. "It will be of no use once we cross the threshold." She hears me but is adamant and continues her chant.

Bronik looks over his shoulder at us, his brow

raised in question. His impenetrable gaze locks to mine, and in defiance, I stare back. I hide the involuntary shiver his presence forces upon my body until he finally turns away without saying a word.

Tatiana completes her chant, and a sky-blue orb surrounds us. The angels don't react because they can't see it—only the witches can. The queen, also a witch, lives in the enchanted castle that will shield her from any danger, including us and our spell.

Upon entering the quad, my sister grips my hand through bound hands, holding it tightly.

Those mingling throughout the markets stop and stare, their curiosity overcoming their typical fear of the angels. We are a low-key family, but after this, there is no doubt that we will quickly become the talk of town.

The castle looms ahead, and due to the scrutinous stares, I am almost happy to arrive. Tatiana, being the same age as the queen, grew up with her. She was known as Veronica back then. They were neighbors for many years and taught each other spells and incantations. They crushed on the same boys and grew competitive as they got older. And then, without warning, Veronica's abilities increased tenfold, and virtually overnight, she became Queen of Cardia and other realms. She suddenly possessed abilities other witches, including Tatiana, simply could not match.

Which was surprising considering Tatiana had always been better at her craft than Veronica growing up.

The castle, set halfway up the hill, which has taken us half a day to get to, is old, its previous owners being the vampires. Its Baroque theme is dark and heavy, the snarling, long-taloned gargoyles poised on top giving the exterior an intimidating air. It suited the vampires, but it is certainly no home for a witch. Not a good one, anyway.

We stop within a few yards of the wooden entry and our protection orb wobbles under the strain of the witch's spell over the castle. The angel leading the way knocks on the door, then steps back into formation and waits. A few heartbeats later, the giant wooden doors creaks open and we are bathed in bright light.

"Move, witches," an angel behind us barks.

Tatiana casts me a worried look, and I'm sure my expression mirrors hers. Squeezing my hand tighter until it hurts, we cross the threshold and watch the blue orb quiver one last time before completely dissolving.

We are defenseless, and I swear Tatiana's shoulders sag in defeat. Our magic could not overthrow the queen, but if we leave here unscathed or even make it back out the door, we will consider ourselves fornunate.

Inside is a vastly different story from the outside. It

isn't old. It isn't intimidating. Instead, everything is pristine white, from the walls to the furniture. Ornate urns dot the perimeter, and traditional Baroque paintings grace the walls. An exquisite chandelier hangs over the middle of the ballroom, casting a golden glow on everything that surrounds us. Compared to how the rest of the wards live, it's clear how our exorbitant rent payments are being used.

We are marched farther into the room and are stopped just shy of a single lounge chair. It's then we see her. Tanya is on her knees, her hands tied tightly behind her back, keeping her still and upright. Her hair is tousled and her face reddened. She looks fearful when her eyes meet mine, instantly rousing the pit of dread in my stomach. Once hopeful we could rescue her, those thoughts are now dashed.

Tatiana, consumed with a desperate need to get to our sister, struggles against the ropes tying her to the angel. Fed up with her futile attempts, the angel yanks on the rope, sending Tatiana hurtling backward. His action looks subtle, but with an angel's strength, it packs a punch. My sister lands harshly on her backside, groaning upon impact.

"That really wasn't necessary," I snap, bending down to help Tatiana to her feet.

"It's real simple," the angel snarls, "she's tied to me for a reason. And that reason is not to run off."

Releasing my sister, I square off with the brutish-looking angel. "We haven't done anything wrong. Therefore we are not your *prisoners*!"

He smiles cruelly and with loathing. "Sure looks like you are to me."

"Let them go to their sister," a familiar voice orders from behind.

I watch the smile fade from the angel's face, his grip tightening on the rope.

I turn to Bronik, whose jaw is set like stone. "Thank you," I offer, but he says nothing.

With a shove to the back, the angel steers Tatiana toward Tanya. I follow, eager to get us all together. As if to taunt her, the angel restrains her when she's only a yard away, preventing Tatiana from consoling our sister.

"Let me go," she hisses, lashing out behind her, and I hear the angel's laugh before he releases the rope. Tanya begins to cry when we both fall to our knees beside her.

"I'm so sorry," she begins between sobs. "I tried to run."

Tatiana's face softens and she smiles weakly. She wants to offer her comfort, but it isn't the time nor place. What matters is that we are all together, and we'll face this as one.

"That's enough," the angel orders before pulling Tatiana to her feet.

She has reached her boiling point and spins to face him, lifting up onto her toes to get closer to his face. "What. Is. Your. Problem?" she seethes.

Again, we see that wicked smile, then his eyes flick to something behind us. "She is your problem."

We don't need to look to know why the hairs on our arms are standing on end. We don't need to look to know the reason for the air around us to have suddenly gone chilling.

"Tatiana," a sing-song voice sounds.

We slowly turn in unison as the queen enters the hall. "Always a pleasure to see you," she croons with obviously false sincerity. She is dressed in an exquisite, red floor-length gown that flows behind her in silken waves. It reminds me of a pool of blood. Like a typical queen, she wears a crown, but it isn't made out of gold and colorful jewels. This one is made out of a circle of rare flowers favored by witches. She walks strong and confident, unfazed by the ropes and tears. There is not even one solicitous glance spared our way as she takes a seat on the pristine white chair in front of us.

"Likewise, my queen," Tatiana says through a smile, yet her teeth are bared. "Can I ask the meaning of you holding us here?"

The queen casts a slow eye over all of us before landing on me. She studies. Watches. Our stares are locked, and I wonder what is going through her pretty head. Most of the world is in fear of her, and maybe a small part of us is as well. But deep down, she is the same witch we grew up with, the one my sister taught a few spells to. So, if I was asked if her stare, the one boring into me right now, is intimatding, I would tell you no. Not in the slightest. Her mouth stays closed, then, finally, she breaks the hold and turns back to Tatiana. "You all look so much alike, yet so different. I forgot that." She talks like she's chiding herself. And then, so abruptly it's unnerving, her expression changes. It darkens. All familiarity is lost. A friendship that survived years is now forgotten. She stands strong and tall, eyes blazing in accusation as she locks eyes with my sister, Tatiana. "Don't you think you have harbored her long enough, Tatiana?"

To my amazement, Tatiana doesn't falter at all. Instead, she too squares her shoulders and accepts the battle. "I'm not following."

The queen scoffs. "Oh, I think you are. And again I ask... don't you think you've kept her secret for far too long?"

"We stay out of everyone's way, and we pay our taxes. We contribute to Cardia without question or resentment. So why are we, all of a sudden, being targeted?"

She is playing a convincing role, and despite having to tame my own boiling rage, I feel an overwhelming sense of pride to have such a strong, determined sister.

The queen makes a tsk sound. "You're always fighting their battles, even when we were young. But now isn't the time, Tatiana. Now is the time for you to take a step back and give what's owed."

"We don't owe anything."

"Oh, you do, so let's just cut to the chase. You know we can never allow the prophecy to come true, and your sister is a threat to making that happen. Cardia is *our* world now. It's all we have left. You do care about the continual rebuild of the earth, don't you? You do care for the air you breathe? For the food you eat?"

It's all lies.

Cardia and its occupants are not endangered. Not by me, anyway. Tatiana knows more than she is letting on. But I know what she knows, and it isn't good. There are reasons why we stay away from other witches, including the queen. We stay away because we know of her betrayal. We know of her allegiance with the demons.

I am indeed included in a prophecy, but I am by no means a threat to others—only the queen.

"So, as a means of protecting the people of Cardia and all we have built after such travesty, Talia is to remain with me. You and Tanya can leave safely and without disturbing the peace. But…" she takes a step forward, pausing before continuing, "…heed my warning. Do not cross me, Tatiana. She may be your sister, but we have so many more lives to think about."

"And her life isn't important? You don't think others will see through these blatant lies of yours? You don't think there will be an uprising? The werewolves don't take too well to deception. They have our backs and—"

"Hush!" the queen spits angrily. "Don't mistake our friendship as leniency. I protect more than just the witches in Cardia, and that includes the wolves."

She gives a small, subtle wave of the hand, and the angels start to gather around, separating me from my sisters. In haste, Tatiana and Tanya stand beside me but are pushed back. I turn to Bronik in panic, but he is deliberately avoiding my gaze.

"Tatiana!" I call when she is dragged farther away.

"Fight, Talia!" she screams. "You need to—" My sister is silenced when a hand covers her mouth, turning her pleas into muffles. She tries to fight her aggressor, but the burley angel is having none of it.

I turn to the witch who looks bored by the whole fiasco. "Tell him to leave her alone," I demand. "Let them go unharmed and I'll stay with you."

Over the chaos, I hear Tanya whimper.

The queen just smiles. Her teeth slowly showing as her mouth widens.

But it's too late.

Tatiana bites down hard on the angel's hand. Losing his temper, his hand wraps around her throat and he throws her backward. It's fast, the force behind it loaded with a super-strength only angels possess.

Tatiana smashes into a white column before falling like a ragdoll and landing heavily on the floor. A snowfall of debris covers her, her eyes barely opening as she lies there unmoving.

My body trembles and tears of frustration spill over my cheeks. I feel a burning rage toward the angels and the queen, and I sense the familiar itch in my hands that only occurs when I'm about to lose control.

Tanya notices and immediately drops to the floor, staying low. She knows what's about to happen and she's taking cover. Her actions cause the angels to raise their brows in question, but it's too late for them to inquire.

A blast of wind circulates through the ballroom, blowing the silken hair of the angels. The queen struggles to tame her red dress, yet I remain unaffected. Those around me shield their eyes as the force grows.

I lock eyes with the angel who hurt Tatiana, and he looks at me curiously, his gaze narrowed as he fights the cyclonic force around him. Raising my hand, I use the power emanating from my gut and hurl the angel backward just like he'd done with my sister. He smashes into the adjacent column, causing a deep fracture that spreads like a vertical vein. Everyone watches with a mixture of surprise and outrage as he falls in a heap to the floor.

All except one.

I hear her voice chanting a spell.

Turning, I watch as the queen moves her hands like she is sculpting clay, words seeking revenge spilling from her mouth.

The floor beneath my feet begins to quake, the tiles rising with jagged edges. Through the broken floor, a portal takes shape and the queen's chant becomes louder.

Tatiana is awake now, her scream catching my attention.

I turn to Bronik, but he is standing too far away, eyes wide as he watches. Did I think he could possibly save me, anyway? Why was there even hope there? The pull of the portal is too strong, and I can't fight it. Clawing at the air in desperation, I feel a hand at the center of my back push me.

"Goodbye," the queen sings in jubilation.

I slip as far down as my waist, and I try in desperation to hoist myself out, but the tiles are cracking under my fingertips as I feel around for leverage.

Then I see the sole of a boot. An angel ready to seal the deal.

Until he doesn't.

He's frozen in place, his boot only inches from connecting with my face.

He doesn't move, and neither does anyone else.

I'm the only one seeing.

Doing.

Until I'm not.

A hand reaches out and hooks under my elbow. In an effortless maneuver, I'm hoisted out of the portal and placed onto steady ground. I'm confronted with a broad chest dressed all in black. I know who it is before my gaze meets his own.

It's him.

It's always been him.

When I brave looking up, I see a smile twitching on his gorgeous face. My heart falters if only for a second. He has always had this effect on me, for as long as I can remember.

He is my own secret.

No one else knows about him, and no one would believe me even if I told them.

I was five when he first came to visit. Appearing out of nowhere to keep me away from danger. And since then, he is a regular visitor, even if it's only from afar. He is the security blanket I never asked for but gladly accept. He's someone I can confide in, someone who never thinks of me as odd or different.

He is just as magnificent-looking as the angels but in a dark, roguish kind of way. There is nothing light about him except for his eyes. Like the angels, they shine a brilliant silver and seem to come to life when I tell him all I have learned for the day.

I know his name, but it wasn't until recently that I found out who he really is. And now, as he stands in from of me, I dread the truth.

His name is Grim.

The Angel of Death.

"I'm not dead!" I say adamantly, running my hands over my body.

Grim simply shakes his head at me. "You bloody well should be, have no doubt about that, my little fighter." He always calls me that, a term of endearment that brings light to a dark situation. I smile until his eyes flick behind me. His affection is lost, and they turn dark at whoever is holding his attention. He can be a frightening man when he is crossed.

"It's not long until they all unfreeze. We have to go." He reaches out and pulls me against his hard chest, his muscled arms wrapping around my body, encasing me. "Snuggle up, fighter."

"Unfreeze them so my sisters can see I'm safe." He

listens and nods his head, and for a second, everything unfreezes.

Confused by what they are witnessing, my sisters watch on. They've never seen Grim before, and now I am leaving with him.

I grip my savior tight and squeeze my eyes closed. There is a moment we are caught in a violent wind, much like the one I created earlier. But it doesn't last longer than a few seconds.

When my eyes reopen, I find myself back in my bedroom. Grim releases me and I'm instantly overcome with dizziness. Transporting as fast as he can carries its consequences for those traveling with him.

"Steady up," he says, gripping my elbow and lowering me to the bed.

"Will that ever get easier?"

"No," he says in all honesty. Grim releases my arm, and I feel him pull away. He is leaving and I feel that familiar pang of loss. "You need to go... *now*. Pack what you can and get to the wolves. They will protect you while I take care of business."

I shake my head. "They won't want any part of this. Defending us against the vampires' hatred is one thing, but taking on the queen and the angels is an entirely different story. They won't want to get caught up in something that could see them banished or killed."

He places a finger underneath my chin, softly with his rough hands, and tilts my face until I meet his hardened gaze. He is having none of it. "The wolves knew about you before you were even born, Talia. They've been expecting this day. They will be ready, and they will fight to keep you safe. Plus, you may be surprised by something when you get there. The alpha *will* protect you."

I'm overcome with sadness, knowing others are placing their lives in danger for me. But I can't let Grim see it. He is strong for me, and I have to be strong for him.

"I will go now," I concede.

A small smile plays on his lips, adding to his handsomeness. "Thank you," is all he says before stepping back and disappearing, leaving me alone. When he leaves me like that, I feel an immediate loss. Like the air has changed and is somehow not as easy to breathe. Why is it easier to breathe when he is here?

To others, the Angel of Death is a mere myth. He doesn't have friends and he doesn't have allies.

He is a man who only appears in your last moments. He knows the good from the bad. And when he comes for you, there is no hiding. There is no pleading for your life. He can take you in an instant once your time is up.

But not with me.

To me, he isn't the Angel of Death. Grim has only ever saved me. He knew of the prophecy, and he will do anything within his power to keep me safe.

I belong to him, and he belongs to me.

I gather a few items of clothing and a choice of weapons, stuffing them all into a black hessian bag. They will all be looking for me, and the house is the first place they will search. But I have one important thing to do first. I run to Tatiana's bedroom and drop to the floor. My nails dig into the wooden plank as I try to unhinge it.

"Come on," I complain, frightened I am wasting too much time. Finally, it raises just enough to hook my fingers under to yank it up and pull Tatiana's diary free. Turning to the page after the last entry, I write my note.

Where our allies lie, there you'll find me.

Closing the book and stuffing it back into the hole in the floor, then sealing it back in place, a chill runs up my spine.

They're coming.

All of them.

Hooking the bag over my shoulder, I take off at a sprint out the back door. If I stay any longer, they will find me. I run fast, meeting the same speed the wolves do when they're on their hunt. I feel eyes burning into the back of me and brave a look. Standing down the street outside my house is Bronik, but he isn't chasing me. Instead, he watches as my feet barely touch the ground in an effort to get as far away as quickly as possible.

He is letting me go.

For whatever reason, he's stopping them from getting to me.

I don't know his intentions.

I don't know if he is setting me up to fail.

Only time will tell whether he is friend or foe.

Chapter Five

The barriers separating the wards are off-limits, and we certainly aren't meant to cross them. But this isn't your average day. The wall is too high. With magic, I could get over it, but that would leave me exposed for others to see. So that only leaves me with one choice. I have to go through the wall, and pushing through objects is never fun for a witch.

Inhaling deeply, I'm ready for a sprint. I close my eyes and imagine I'm falling through a cloud, visualizing it the best I can. Light and transcendent.

Reality is entirely different.

I'm hit with the full force, my body now moving in slow motion as it courses through the thick wall. I feel the pressure bind to my body, until finally, I exit the wall and time speeds up a thousand-fold. That's when

I am sent careening out, my feet unable to keep up with the pace.

I didn't see it coming, but I certainly feel it. A hard body meets mine on impact, and I rebound off, landing heavily on the ground. I'm winded and struggle to catch my breath. Wheezing, feeling my lungs fill with air again, I start dusting myself off.

"That was certainly an entrance," a deep, gravelly voice says, startling me.

A hand reaches down to help, and I meet his gaze. The shifter has a thick head of hair and deep brown eyes. A scar mars his face, but that doesn't take away from his good looks.

"Take my hand, witch," he says, drawing my attention back to him. I accept and he hoists me to my feet. He says nothing more, and at this point, I'm unsure what to say anyway. Maybe Grim was right—the wolves were expecting me. Why else would there be a lone shifter standing at this particular spot of the fence?

I watch as he starts to walk away with no further instruction. I catch up and follow along closely behind him, hoping he will take me where I need to go.

This ward is unfamiliar, and the layout is vastly different from the witches' ward. All is quiet, but I can feel eyes staring at me through their various hiding places. Curtains are pulled to the side ever so slightly, and children peer around trees, their curiosity too much for them not to check out the oddity. Noise suddenly emanates from farther down the street, startling me and making me pause. A group of male shifters is responsible for the ruckus, drinking to the point where they're all having a good time, laughing and oblivious to ward rules.

Maybe their rules are different from ours?

If witches drink, it is at their own risk. Alcohol, especially the raw type found in Cardia, only decreases our powers.

"Keep moving, witch," the shifter orders. Those partying see us walking up the street and stop and stare. They can smell I'm not one of theirs, their noses leading as they detect my distinctive scent.

I quick-step to keep pace with the shifter, and only a block later, he leads me to a house that sits separate from the others. It's on a large block of land with a shed out the back. The entire property is surrounded by lush, green grass, which is entirely different from our ward.

We come to a stop and another shifter comes into view. He's shirtless, leaning over the engine of a car. Cars aren't used in Cardia. This is the first one I've ever seen and I doubt it works. The shifter's muscles move beautifully in time with every action, his skin sun-kissed. I watch while he uses a rag to rub grease off some part of the machinery and then to clean his hands.

Finally, he turns and eyes us both.

"Why are you in my territory, witch?" he asks, his voice deep but calm and steady. He has to be the alpha of the pack.

"I'm in trouble."

He shrugs his shoulders. "What business is that of mine?"

"I needed to escape, and I know the wolves can help."

"You just assume we can help? That we want to help?"

I'm not deterred. Wolf shifters carry an arrogance around with them wherever they go. It's ingrained behavior. They are confident, arrogant, and often to others, it would be deemed rude. I know better. Or should I say, I was told better.

"We've helped each other for thousands of years. Now is no different."

He drops the cloth on the car and meets me head-on. "Now is vastly different. Cardia is a new world and nothing like the one where our allegiance was formed."

"The queen is after me."

This gets his attention.

He pauses, lost in thought.

"Why is the queen after you?" I watch his thumb tap on his thigh.

"She believes I am a threat to her."

"And are you?"

"Maybe."

He considers me a moment, knowing I'm not divulging everything. "Are you the one from the prophecy?"

"Yes."

His jaw tightens, his thumb twitch becoming more aggressive. "So, it's all true?" He asks the question more to himself. "With as much destruction as it will bring, it will also give us hope. Her reign will be no more."

"Maybe." I can't be certain if that is how things are going to unfold. I'm a novice at this.

He steps forward until we are toe-to-toe. Wearing a frown, he sniffs around my face. He recoils immediately, wearing a scowl. His hands enclose on my face, lifting it to meet his. His sky-blue eyes are rimmed with red as he studies me closely.

"Who was the last to touch you?"

I swallow hard under his scrutiny. Lying to a werewolf is not acceptable. Especially while standing in their ward.

"An angel."

"No, a woman. Tell me of her," he demands, practically growling.

"The queen," I reply, remembering feeling her hand on my back.

"No, I know her scent, it is not her. Another?" he insists.

"My sister. She and I walked together. She held my hand."

His eyes lock on my hand, then they seem lost in a world I don't understand. When he looks past me to the other shifter and nods, I wonder what his interest is in my sister's scent.

"What's your name?" he asks, now back to business.

"Talia."

"Well, Talia, I welcome you to our ward."

Chapter Six

The night's festivities are unlike anything I've ever experienced. A bonfire blazes in a field, its orange and golden embers drifting in the breeze like tiny stars. Those of the werewolf ward dance jovially around the fire, a mere strip of cloth barely covering their bodies.

John, the alpha, sits close to me, but not close enough that we are touching. Every now and then he casts a sideward glance my way. His mouth opens slightly as if to say something, but then he turns away with a slight shake of his head.

The ward is hospitable, offering me something to drink. Although I politely say no, the shifters turn their noses up in disgust. Drinking and being merry is a part of what they do. Every day is a celebration. But to a witch, our abilities weaken when we drink, and I am in no position right now to have any of my power diminished.

While the others lose themselves to the rhythm and heat from the fire, I battle with the thoughts plaguing me. I worry for my sisters and whether they have made it home unharmed. I worry how far the queen will go to find me. I worry that when I close my eyes at night, I will wake up seeing her wicked, smiling face.

I feel hopeless.

Beside me, John clears his throat.

"For goodness' sake, just ask me," I declare, exasperated by his odd behavior. He once again looks at me, but this time he appears slightly nervous.

"What does she look like?" He breaks eye contact, his voice is uneven, and I can't help but smile.

"We all look similar... dark hair, green eyes."

"Are you all alike?" This time he holds my gaze, and that's when I see just how interested he is in finding out more about my sister.

"No, Tatiana is the eldest. She's more of the protector, I guess you could say. She trains us, keeps us on schedule, and maintains the house. Sometimes, I think she has to be like our parents. Tanya, on the other hand, is the peacemaker. She doesn't like having to fight for everything, especially something as basic as our safety."

I smile as their faces come to mind. This is the first

time I have been separated from my sisters, and it feels strange having to describe them in this way.

Beside me, I doubt John listened to a word I said from the faraway look on his face.

"Tatiana." He lets her name roll off of his tongue like he is getting used to hearing and saying it.

I'm almost lost in my own thoughts when the hairs on my body stand on end. My senses come on high alert, and instinctively, I grip John's arm. He looks at it, then follows my worried gaze.

"They're coming!"

"Where?" John is quick to his feet, pulling me up with him. He is strong and powerful, and it is easy to feel safe in his presence. But that doesn't mean the threat isn't real.

As if on cue, those dancing around the bonfire come to a standstill. They can sense my fear. Wary faces meet ours, and it's then I notice John's eyes are now glowing orange. His shoulders square for battle and his pack quickly follow suit.

All their eyes are now glowing a bright yellow. Since John is the alpha, his color is different. It distinguishes him from the rest.

"Where are they?" he asks again.

To feel their presence, I close my eyes and point in the direction of the threat, and all gazes follow.

John releases my arm, and taking a few steps forward, he sniffs the air, hoping to pick up any trace.

"I can't smell them."

"They are close to the border." My voice trembles slightly. I'm scared. The anticipation from everything that's happened today has me on edge. The expectancy of what's to come has me tense and nervous. My body tenses, my hands becoming clammy.

"Tell me more."

"I can feel my sister. She's... she is there somewhere. Somewhere close. They are with Tatiana."

John's back straightens at the mention of her name, and he nods to Patrick, the one I met at the brick wall when I first arrived. Patrick comes right over and stands tall in front of me. He himself is a brick wall and I feel miniature in his presence.

"Get her to safety," John instructs in a low, calm voice. Without hesitating, Patrick takes my arm, but I try to pull free. I manage to twist out of his grasp, and he is surprised by my strength.

"I can help!" I tell them, but they will have nothing of it.

The others are beginning to shift into their wolf forms, and it's a mesmerizing transition—so beautiful and elegant, yet terrifying at the same time.

John's attention, however, is still focused on trying to locate the threat.

"You need to leave... so *leave*," Patrick demands, once again gripping my arm. This time his fingers dig deep into the muscle to the point where it hurts. He leads the way, dragging me from the light of the bonfire and into the darkness. He is fast, but I keep up, and soon my eyes adjust to the mirky blackness around me.

The wolves howl and it echoes through the night, so I stop to witness the spectacle. Hyped and ready for battle, I see them in their pack, but then I see shapes move so fast, I have to blink to make sure what I am witnessing is real.

Vampires.

"Come on," Patrick urges, his voice deep and serious this time. "We can't stop. They will smell you. We have to leave."

I know he's right. A mere breeze could carry my scent and it would be game over. The problem is, I'm transfixed. I can't move—my attention solely on John.

A vampire stands face to face with John, but John doesn't shift an inch. He's poised in the face of evil.

"Why isn't he moving?" I ask, turning back to Patrick, whose eyes are glowing a bright yellow.

"John has no reason to be afraid. He could kill two of them without even shifting. And then when he does shift, all hell will break loose."

Patrick speaks with such high confidence about his

pack leader that when he takes my arm again, I follow without hesitation.

That is until I hear her voice.

Coming to a grinding halt, I turn back to the fire. Tatiana is being dragged by two vampires, one snapping his teeth at her ear, taunting her. Having messed with the wrong person, not being one to take taunts lying down, she snaps her head to the side before whipping it back into his. Knowing Tatiana and her strength, it would have hurt. I watch the vampire stagger backward as a result. Not one to be made a fool of, he quickly rights himself and slaps her hard across the cheek. The vamps can move so fast that their actions can easily go undetected. Like right now, Tatiana cops the full force, barely with time to see what is happening.

My skin tingles with adrenaline, and I take off running, engaging my full speed. Behind me, Patrick follows, struggling to keep pace, his cursing barely reaching my ears. I only have one thing in mind, and that is saving my sister.

Tatiana's hands are bound behind her back, and in that position, her magic is restricted. She'll only be able to fight back physically, and that won't be enough to stop the vampires. I emerge from the darkness and am at her side before the others even notice. At the same time, John launches himself at the vampire who struck Tatiana. He shifts mid-air, losing his human form and transforming into his powerful alpha wolf. His mouth, wide and angry, latches on to the vampire's neck, tearing his head straight off. The decapitated body falls heavily to the ground next to us.

Tatiana, who remains largely unfazed, kicks at the vamp's hand that landed by her foot. I, on the other hand, having been protected by my sister all my life, am frozen in place. I'm shocked by the brutality of the necessary attack, it being unlike anything I've ever witnessed.

Hissing and seething with rage, the other three vampires sprint toward us.

I fall to the ground, sinking my fingers into the soft earth. I feel the others around me—Tatiana, Patrick, and John—and when they are safe, I release my power and brace as the ground violently quakes until it finally splits like an angry fork toward the vampires who try to stumble out of its path.

But it's too late.

A new fork in the earth opens and the vamps slip over, clawing desperately at the edge. With a final shake, they all fall, disappearing forever. Keeping my hands in place, lying flat on the ground, I watch as the earth begins to heal itself, the open wounds closing to form a fresh, tight seal.

"Talia." I faintly hear my name. "Talia, come back to us. Come back."

Two soft hands touch my arms from behind, raising me to my feet. My trembling body is encased in a warm embrace, and I can feel the magic ebbing, allowing me to see straight again. I hold Tatiana, grateful to be reunited with her.

Over her shoulder, I see the stares of John, Patrick, and the rest of the wolves now shifted back to human form. They are wide-eyed and curious, albeit somewhat wary of me.

Mine is a power that can't be tamed.

It is a power that, if in the wrong hands, could be devastating to Cardia.

I only hope they see me as a benefit to the cause and not something needing to be ostracized.

At that particular moment, observing their penetrating glares, my world and everything in it turns black.

I hear talking, but the voices turn to yelling.

I wake, barely, and feel arms wrapped around me. They're strong and protective, and when I move, he holds me tighter.

My eyes gradually open and I see we are now

inside. Patrick is cradling me in his lap, keeping my shivering at bay.

At the opposite end of the room, Tatiana is screaming at John, who does nothing but smirk in response. His cocky act only making her crazier. He sees the humor behind it, and she seems fueled by his behavior. In a half-hearted attempt, I make a move to shut her up, but Patrick prevents me.

"Rest," is all he says, pulling me close against his warm body. After another few minutes, and fed up with the feud playing out in front of me, I stand on shaky legs. Tatiana notices and runs to my side.

"Don't do that again unless you absolutely have to," she chastises, clearly upset with me.

My eyes bulge open.

No thank you.

No anything.

"We had it handled," she continues, seeing my reaction. "Mr. Know-It-All over there..." she grumbles, her thumb indicating to John, "...could have destroyed them."

With a smile, he takes a step closer to her until his chest hovers slightly over her back. I watch curiously as my sister's breath catches in response to John's nearness. She can feel how close he is, and I'm not sure what is transpiring. Just a moment ago, she wanted to beat his head in, and now, she's lost in his presence.

"Where is Tanya?" I ask in an attempt to bring everyone back to the present issue at hand.

Tatiana drops her head at the sound of our sister's name, and it's then I notice the bruises over her arms and neck.

"The angels have her still," she admits, and a familiar rage courses through me. "I was allowed to leave..." she continues, "...because they believed you seeing me would bring you back."

I remain quiet, lost in thought as I plan my attack.

"Who was he, Talia?" Tatiana questions me with a slight edge to her tone that I don't appreciate. "There are whispers about him. Is it true? Is he... the Angel of Death?"

I nod slowly, and realization dawns on her pretty face.

"He is the Angel of Death," I confirm.

"Then why did he save you, Talia? That's not his role. The Angel of Death doesn't save anyone. He takes away. What haven't you been telling me?" I can feel everyone watching our tense interaction. Since it affects them, they, too, need answers. But Tatiana can sense my hesitation and turns to John. "We need some privacy," she instructs with a hand on her hip.

My sister is bossy by nature, but John simply looks at her like she is the only one in the room. He isn't fazed by her unwarranted aggression. Instead, he takes it in his stride, like he enjoys the challenge. I'm sure it isn't every day a woman stands equal to him. The room clears with a few mutters and groans, but when it's empty, my sister folds her arms and waits for me to continue talking.

"I've known him forever," I admit, and her eyes go wide.

"How? I don't understand. How is that even possible?" She shakes her head, adamant she's missing something. "He was able to control the angels with such ease. No one has been able to do that, and now you're telling me that the Angel of Death has been by your side your whole life?"

"Yes." My answer is simple but effective.

Tatiana exhales heavily. I never told her because she would never have believed me. Just like now.

"He is the Angel of Death, Talia. This isn't something to treat lightly."

"I'm well aware of that. He protects me. He would never let anything happen to me. He's kept me safe my whole life, and then once again yesterday."

She looks unconvinced, like I'm covering for him.

"He. Is. The. Angel. Of. Death," she reiterates slowly, succinctly.

"I know!" I'm exasperated by the whole discussion. I know she needed to know, but she wasn't open to the truth at the time and I haven't felt at any time up until now that she would even listen to me.

It isn't until I follow Tatiana's gaze over my shoulder that I realize no one will understand the relationship between me and the one they fear most. They think of him as a myth. Since those who see him never live long afterward to tell their story, he has always been feared should your time come to an end.

Now, it seems he is a lot closer than they all thought.

Death is coming for us all.

Chapter Seven

Tatiana is breathing lightly next to me, still sound asleep. After our discussion the night before, we—especially me—were completely drained and in need of rest. When used, my magic expels too much energy, and my recovery time is essential. Without pushing me further with her inquiry, I put the night's horrors to the recesses of my mind and fell asleep before I even closed my eyes.

Sitting up, I spy John by the door, his gaze flicking between the happenings outside, keeping watch, and a slumbering Tatiana. My curiosity has been piqued.

"Why are you so interested in her?" I ask, keeping my voice low. If she knew we were talking about her, we'd all be in trouble.

John simply shakes his head. "She knows why." A small smile plays on his lips.

I look down to my sleeping sister, then back to him. "This tension between you is driving us all insane. I've never seen anyone have this effect on her. She won't tell me. She avoids the question when I ask. So... tell me. What is going on?"

John rubs his jawline, suddenly nervous to be talking. "She is my mate," he says with pride.

His response surprises me, so much so, that saliva catches in my throat, and I start to cough.

"Wha—?" I barely manage. "She isn't a werewolf," I exclaim, feeling like I have to state the obvious.

"I know she's a witch."

"Well, isn't that where the issue is? She isn't a werewolf, so how can she be your mate?"

John shakes his head. "Not necessarily. I'm an alpha, and none of the women here can match my needs, match my power." We both look to Tatiana, and I'm surprised to see she's now awake and hearing everything we've been saying. Her eyes are still closed but a small smile plays on her lips, which is a dead giveaway.

"I didn't believe it either, until I saw her," John continues. "I need someone who can lead with me, and that someone needs to be strong and confident. I've been on this earth for hundreds of years, and not once have I even come close to finding a woman like her. Until now." John rises and makes to leave, but before he exits, he turns, a megawatt smile on his face.

"You can get up now, Tatiana," he teases before walking out.

I look to Tatiana and she rolls her eyes. "Can you believe him?" She huffs, sitting up. "Like I will ever be his mate and howl at the moon with the bloody wolves." Flicking the blanket to the side, she strides to the bathroom with a skip in her step. My sister is behaving particularly out of character, almost as if she is enjoying the idea of being a mate and the flirtation that goes with that fact.

"Is it true?" I ask while she washes her face. Were-wolves and mating aside, we have a more important issue to discuss. "About demons. Is it true that the queen made a deal with them?"

"If angels are real, I don't see why demons can't exist. I haven't personally seen one, but she couldn't have gotten that powerful all on her own." Tatiana leans against the bathroom doorframe, arms crossed. "While we were growing up, her powers were far weaker than mine. But now I can't even chant near her without her interfering and breaking the spell."

She pulls her hair back and wraps it in a bun. When finished with her own hair, she comes back to the bed where I'm still sitting and runs her fingers through my loose tresses. When she starts to braid it, I lean back against her legs and relax. She doesn't do this often, only when she wants to concentrate, so I don't talk or disturb her as she goes. Then, when I feel the last pull, I look up at her.

"We have to go to the vampires," she says, and my horrified expression meets hers.

Has she gone completely insane?

Is her newfound love affecting her cognitive ability?

Witches don't ever set foot into the vampire ward. Not ever.

"We need to summon the demon that helped the queen, and the only place to do that is near their castle at the crossroads."

"No fucking way!" a voice booms from the doorway, and we both jump in fright at the mighty sound. Now minus a t-shirt, all muscles glistening with sweat, John takes up almost the entire opening. His eyes glow a bright orange, his jaw set like stone.

"Will you stop that and put on a shirt," Tatiana chides, waving at his bare chest. She may have tried to flip off his assertiveness, but there is an unmistakable pink glow on her cheeks. She likes him, and for whatever reason, she feels the need to keep him at bay.

"You can't go anywhere unless I go with you," he asserts, and Tatiana scoffs. She wriggles out from behind me and stands head-on with John, preparing for battle.

"Please! You are *not* my father, and we certainly

don't answer to you or need you to escort us anywhere."

Having none of it, John takes two steps forward, his dominating physique filling the room. His broad, tanned chest is right in her face. She has to look up to see him, and I can tell that was his intention.

"It's not up for discussion," he says in a slow rumble that even makes me still. "Wherever *you* go, *I* go. Do you know why?" Tatiana opens her mouth to answer, but he cuts her off. "Now that my mate has finally shown herself, I won't let you leave my side."

Her small hands push against his chest, but he doesn't budge, not even an inch. This only adds to her frustration, so she tries again, this time with double the force. John snatches at her hands, yanking her close. A tiny squeal escapes her lips, her eyes hooded with desire I've never seen before.

"I'm going to kiss you very soon, and the last thing you will do is push me away. Do you know why *that* is? Because you will like it and you will scream for more."

Good Lord!

Scooting out of bed and edging around the two, I make an escape outside before I witness anything more disturbing. My exit goes unnoticed, their lustful eyes only for each other.

I get as far away from the house as possible until I can no longer hear their voices. Tilting my head up to the bright yellow sun, I close my eyes and absorb the warmth steaming down around me.

"You're looking better," a deep voice pulls me from my reverie.

Reluctantly, I open my eyes to Patrick. He is at my side and gestures for me to follow him on a walk. There is silence between us while we take in the freshness of the morning. We were lucky in Cardia. This didn't exist back where our family came from. We had ruined it.

"You think she will make a good leader?" I finally ask, breaking the silence.

"Your sister's power rivals his. No one, especially a female, has ever rivaled him. So yes, I do think they'll work. Even if others are counting on them not to."

"Why would they think that?"

"The same reason you do. She's not a wolf, so you can't comprehend how it will work. We only shift when we absolutely need to, though. So, they are more alike than you think." Patrick pauses, looking around the ward at the houses. "Some of the women here have tried their best to gain his attention, but he could tell just by their scent that they wouldn't even get close to his side."

As if on cue, a scream sounds from John's house, causing the women in the area to stare longingly, pondering what must be happening.

What is happening?

I stop, looking between the house and Patrick.

"Relax." He chuckles. "They're just having fun. John won't let up until Tatiana joins his side."

The women who have been watching begin gossiping amongst each other, and I immediately feel uncomfortable. We don't need enemies. There are too many of those chasing us already.

"They're just not used to the idea of a witch climbing the ladder so quickly," Patrick chimes in. With his hand at the small of my back, he steers me down the road.

"Have you been there? To the vampires' ward?" I ask, sitting down on a large log by the bonfire pit. Small embers continue to glow, not having enough power to turn into a flame.

"No, I haven't, but John has. He was the only one to make it out alive many years ago."

A shiver spreads through me at the thought of the bloody battles between the wards.

Chapter Eight

Patrick leaves me with my thoughts to attend to his duties. Like the witches, the wolves have their own roles to play to keep their ward running smoothly.

I hear the slight crunch of footsteps behind me, but I don't need to turn to know who it is. It's easy to identify based on their stride. Tatiana takes a seat next to me on the log, bringing with her the heated stares from the females in the pack.

They are looking for a weakness. A reason to pounce. A reason to have us removed. And all because Tatiana had somehow become the chosen mate of the alpha. Her new life, should she choose to live it, will mean her love for solitude would exist no more. She is strong and confident. But being a witch in a wolf pack she doesn't know? A wolf pack that so far hasn't taken too well to her? I don't know how she will live without changing a huge part of herself in order to fit in.

She is my strength, and I'm not ready to lose her so soon and unexpectedly. Sensing my fears, Tatiana places a hand on my shoulder, and it brings the usual comfort. I calm instantly, and we settle into an easy silence, still exhausted from the night's events.

I'm first to talk, keen to put the witch hunt at the back of our minds, if only for a moment.

"I can feel your rage." I smile.

Beside me, Tatiana sighs heavily. "He's just so..." She closes her eyes and faces me, shaking her head. "Never mind."

"Come on. Tell me," I urge.

"This predicament is difficult to wrap my head around. Not for hundreds of years has this happened. Wolves and witches have little in common. I can't see how this will work. I'm not one of *them*."

"But it has happened in the past, and it will continue to happen. It's happening to you right now, and I think you need to explore it. A wolf's scent is never wrong. And besides..." I pause, stopping my smile from spreading farther, "...it's not like the witches' ward is loaded with prospects."

Tatiana giggles at the understatement. The truth is, there are no viable options for the witches. Becoming the mate of a wolf—a hot wolf at that—is the best thing that could happen to Tatiana.

"He thinks he owns me already," she scoffs with mock indignation. Being "owned" is a difficult concept for my headstrong sister to even entertain.

"Already?" I question. "It's been less than a day."

She looks at me with large eyes, lips twitching as she envisions her mate. "I won't lie, he's hot, and I haven't seen or been attracted to anyone, for... like... *ever*. But at the same time, he makes my blood boil. His ego—"

"You have an ego, too," I quip. I'm rewarded with a gentle elbow to the ribs.

"He's just so cocky and self-assured, but he makes me feel other things at the same time." Sensing his presence, she turns away from me and watches John leave his house. He's still bare-chested with taut muscles on glorious display. It's no wonder all the women around here pant after him. He brings it on himself.

Yet, unlike all the other women who fall at his feet, Tatiana grumbles, but she doesn't look away.

"If only he would get over his barbaric ways." With her forgetting how in-tune they are, John stops in his tracks and locks eyes with her. He's smiling, having heard every word she said even though he's far from earshot.

"I think you like it, a lot," I whisper low, determined not to sink my sister in further. She's quite capable of doing that herself.

"You may be right, but that isn't my focus." She turns to face me, eyes suddenly serious. "You are."

I nod my head but am at a loss for words. Perhaps I'm too frightened to express my concerns. She senses my unease and tries a different approach. "Now, tell me more about the Angel of Death. He certainly has eyes only for you."

What does she mean by that?

"Grim protects me. He always has. Where he is the Angel of Death for some, to me, he has only ever kept me safe."

Tatiana scrunches her brows together, uncertain of how she should interpret the relationship I have with Grim.

"He comes to me at the most unexpected times," I continue. "He knows when I need him most, and he's never let me down. I can count on him."

"He saved you, Talia!" I see a glimmer of hope in her eyes. Having Grim on my side during this time is a huge asset. One that will surely ebb some worry off my sister's mind. "He stopped you from going through the portal, only the Angel of Death has that power... to stop time." She pauses, taking a deep breath. "We are going into incredibly dangerous territory tonight. If you need him again, will he come for you?"

It is never as simple as that.

"History tells me yes. Yes, he will be there. But... I don't call to him. I don't even know how to. He simply appears. He knows what's going on before I do."

"I can only hope he can go into battle with us. Become our ally. We will need all the help we can get. I trust in the wolves, but even they are not strong enough to defeat the queen and her army. The Angel of Death is the only one who carries power to rival that of the other angels and whatever the queen can muster. He can control the elements, stop time, and travel back through it. He can outsmart the other angels because they work for the queen and act on her behalf. He is a lone soldier. He answers to no one and has no duty to uphold. That makes him as beneficial as he is dangerous."

I see the worry in her eyes. The uncertainty of whether she can place her trust in the Angel of Death to protect her sister—and her, for that matter.

"Don't get me wrong..." she continues, "...we witches have some tricks up our sleeves, and the wolves are a solid army. But we need Grim to step up and be there."

"Girls." John's voice sounds from behind us. We turn and watch as he pulls a shirt over his tanned, muscled torso. "The sun isn't going to be up forever. We need to move."

"Okay, we will prepare," Tatiana responds with zero hostility, which renders both John and myself speechless. Curious glances are thrown between us, but my sister seems none the wiser of her extreme mood swings toward John. One minute, she's rebelling against every look and every word, the next, she is cooperating with a smile on her pretty face.

Tatiana stands from the log. Taking my hands in hers, she sits us both on the ground. To build strength, we utilize the power the earth offers us and embrace it as a coven. Or in this case, just my sister and me. We close our eyes and let the warmth of the sun heat our skin, inhaling deeply, feeling the soil and its richness beneath us. She taught me all this when I was younger. I do this more for Tatiana's sake, since she relies on the earth's energy to build and maintain her powers. Tatiana's power is earth.

"We need to go, now," she instructs while getting to her feet. When she's focused, nothing gets in the way. Tatiana has already walked away, starting our journey, when I begin to follow. Patrick nudges John as she strides past, and he simply smiles. He is so smitten with my sister that it is almost sickening. Five other men join us as we begin our trek to the other ward, which will consume most of the day. Less if we don't have to watch our backs with every step we take. Sundown is our mark, harnessing the moon's power as it begins its ascension.

I stealthily watch the shifters that surround us, their sheer size dwarfing me. With strong, broad shoulders displaying their dominance, the shifters are a powerful force to be reckoned with. And here they are, protecting two witches they barely know, all because of a long-standing alliance between our ancestors. They are willing to risk their own lives for us, and for that I feel an overwhelming pride in them.

We all stop in front of the ward but are blocked by the wall that's in place during hours no one can leave. Each ward is granted leave for only a few hours a day to access the market. Now is not that time.

Tatiana steps forward, letting her raised palms hover inches away from the wall in an effort to push back against the power preventing us from leaving. It wobbles and sways while she silently mouths a chant. Beads of sweat drip down her temples, and I know she is losing too much energy by doing this. The wards are controlled by the queen, and her energy is far greater than Tatiana's. I step in line next to her and mirror her hands, channeling my strength to push through the spell. Within a heartbeat, a large circle of the wall moves, from wobbles to waves, and then quickly begins to evaporate. My sister casts me a wide-eyed glance, watching for my own health as we demolish the wall. She knows the extent of my power, but would rather I keep my reserve for when it's required.

"Go now," she orders to the werewolves, who begin to one by one step through the hole we have made. John and Patrick remain behind, wanting to ensure we are safe.

Tatiana will have none of it. "Go," she demands again.

I nod to John who seems to carry the same thoughts as me. He's fast and she hasn't a chance to stop it. John wraps his hands around Tatiana's hips, pulling her through the hole. She squeals before he stands her straight down on the other side of the wall. She looks back through to me and I know time is of the essence. Stepping one leg through, the hole begins to close with the sudden loss of power. Warm hands wrap around my forearm, and I'm yanked all the way until I collide once again with Patrick's broad chest.

My groan is followed by his deep chuckle. He straightens me and a megawatt smile lights up his face.

"Second time's a charm," he jokes, forcing a smile from me.

"Thank you," I offer, knowing that despite some hostility among the wolves, Patrick has a good heart.

Past Patrick, I see laughing eyes holding my gaze. Tatiana is grinning knowingly, and I frown at her suggestion there is something between Patrick and me. Anything to keep the focus off her own relationship squabbles. She is shameless.

The group proceeds forward, and it's easy to see how the wolves fall into formation within their pack. Tatiana and John take the lead up front and walk in silence. No doubt each of them is contemplating our plan of attack.

And then the peace is interrupted with a voice that chills me to the bone. A voice that cajoles with a menace that's undeserved.

A voice calling my name.

Talia.

Tatiana hears it too and comes to an immediate stop. She turns on her heel, eyes wide in worry, and strides toward me.

Talia, the voice sounds again.

The wolves look curiously at our changed demeanor but are unable to hear the voice calling out.

I don't have to look around and search the area for its source. The voice is other-worldly. Targeted specifically for me.

My, my, my. Aren't you a pretty little thing? The voice practically purrs.

There is no denying its wicked intentions.

"Who is that?" Tatiana asks me with a shake in her voice. She grips my hands, and by now, the wolves have come to a stop and are watching our interaction. Her cautious eyes dart around the area, looking for whoever's doing the taunting.

"They're not here," I say, squeezing her hands with reassurance.

"Do you know who it is?"

"No. I don't recognize the voice."

John approaches from behind, his brows knit in confusion.

"What voice?" he asks, looking between us. "I didn't hear anything."

You think the big bad wolf can save you? The question is followed by a manic laugh, a promise of things to come.

Tatiana jumps in fright as she looks desperately around.

The wolves start circling. Waiting for some indication of what is transpiring.

He can't save you and neither can his pack. You are simply leading them to their deaths.

"Who are you?" Tatiana commands angrily, surprising John. "Don't be a coward. Show yourself."

Such bravery, but oh so stupid.

The voice is taunting, and I've just about had enough. "What do you want?"

There is a bounty on you, Talia. The queen is awaiting your arrival.

"The queen will *not* win!" I yell.

That's what you think. The warning is followed by another bone-chilling laugh.

"Can someone explain to us what is happening right now?" John all but demands.

Stupid, stupid wolves. The voice has turned almost metallic. Sharp and sinister. *He will be the first to die.*

Tatiana's hand flings out, gripping his arm and pulling him close. He studies her reaction but remains silent.

"You can't hurt us," my sister spits, determined not to be shaken. "We're strong together."

Even with a traitor among you? The voice sounds like it is smiling, having identified a weakness within the group.

Watch who you trust, Talia.

"It's not true," I whisper to Tatiana. This thing is just playing mind tricks on us.

There is a silence, and we all wait on a knife's edge for the next blow. Tatiana's eyes flick to mine, her knuckles turning white on John's arm.

A strong gust of wind begins to circle around us, picking up dry earth, leaves, and branches. My long hair whips in my eyes and I shield my face from the debris. Struggling against the force, we gather in a huddle, leaning against each other for support, and wait it out.

When the wind finally ebbs and we've dusted ourselves off, we are delivered a final warning.

Let the games begin.

"What do we do now?" Tatiana's eyes flick to me, loaded with apprehension.

"We keep moving forward."

"What did you hear?" John asks.

"A voice," I simply reply.

"Whose voice?"

"I don't know, exactly. A vampire, most likely."

I move around them to continue the journey, and the others fall into step, their questions ongoing.

"You both look pretty shaken up," John observes. "Tell us what the voice said."

"The vampires know we are coming and will be waiting. The queen has a bounty on my head." The words fall from my mouth.

"How do they know you're coming? We've only just started the journey."

This time I stop in my tracks and face him with seriousness written all over my face. "They said a wolf from this pack told them. That I should be careful who I trust."

Immediately, I feel heat radiating toward me. The wolves don't appreciate this type of talk, and I understand their anger.

John curses under his breath before eyeing his

pack. They stand still, keeping their gazes focused on their leader, every one of them assertive with their shoulders squared.

Then he looks back at me, shaking his head. "It's none of them," he says adamantly. "I trust everyone here with my life."

"I don't doubt," I reassure.

We continue on, and I listen to John and Patrick discuss what happened and the potential issues we could now face. With each step I take, the castle on the mountain becomes clearer. Next to it, the moon is beginning its ascension.

The vampires will be waiting for us once the moon is high in the night sky, and I'm not even sure a pack of wolves and two witches will be able to fight them off for long. The wolves are strong and powerful and should be feared, but the vampires are quick and agile and use the power of manipulation to their advantage. They could cast a hypnotic spell with just the sound of their silken voice.

The vampires' ward is closest to the castle, but the demon crossing is located between them. That is our destination—a risky mission with two enemies having us as their target. We need to summon the demon who bears a long-standing agreement with the queen before a bloody battle ensues.

We navigate the streets through the quad, keeping

to the shadows and avoiding the moonlit areas. My palms are sweating, and as soon as I wipe them on my pants they begin to sweat once more. The closer we come to our destination, the more anxious I become.

We are walking behind a wall when John raises his hand, signaling for us to stop.

I move closer to his side, bypassing the other wolves, and look to where he is pointing.

"It's just over there," he says. "Between the rock wall of the castle and the neighboring ward." Ahead is the point where the two roads meet at the junction.

Summoning a demon is something new to me. I don't even know where to start and have no idea what will come of it. Even if we will walk away alive. Tatiana only knows what she has read, both of us lacking on the practical side of things and the skills that might be required. The *how to use them* covered, the *training and application* sorely lacking.

"Salt?" Tatiana asks Patrick, who's been carrying the bag. He holds it up and John starts the convoy across the remainder of the deserted quad until we reach the crossroad.

"Everyone in a circle," my sister instructs.

The wolves take formation surrounding us as Tatiana sprinkles the salt around her, forming a barrier, then she tilts her head to the sky to begin her chant.

"Hear these words, I summon thee.

With everything in me, I trap thee.
I pay the price requested, I summon thee."

On the last verse she moves her hand in a circular motion in front of her, her voice raising an octave.

"From the depths of hell, I summon thee."

Now complete, she opens her eyes and looks to those looking at her. The wolves are quiet in anticipation, knowing this part of the journey is out of their control. Just like earlier, but without vampire influence, the gentle breeze becomes a gust and we each shield our eyes until he appears.

Within seconds, he is before us.

Standing in the middle of the circle, in all his powerful glory, is the demon himself. He is dressed similarly to that of the Angel of Death, but he carries an air of disturbing sophistication with him. His eyes flash a fiery red before returning to their normal color. They flick with keen interest between me and Tatiana and back to me again. He smiles, and it's the type of smile that promises all the things you never wish for. I shiver, and he delights in my discomfort.

Satisfied, he turns back to the bearer of the spell. "Why do you summon me, witch?" The deep authority with which he speaks makes us all uneasy. His eyes flick to the salt barrier on the ground she created, his lips twitching in amusement. "Salt? Are you frightened of me, witch? Are you worried about what I could do to you in front of all of them?" He casts a glance at the circle of wolves. John's jaw twitches at the threat, but he remains stoic in the face of the demon.

"We need help," Tatiana steers the conversation to the path it should be on.

"And what would a good witch like yourself need from a demon like me?"

"I need information that only you and one other would know."

"Well, doesn't this sound intriguing? And what information would that be, little witch?" he questions, tilting his head to the side to assess her.

"A long time ago, you made a deal with the queen. I want you to tell me what that deal was." Tatiana could woo even the most stoic of opponents. She's always so strong and determined. I can see why John is so drawn to her.

The demon considers her words before once again glancing between us. "I think you already know that deal." His voice takes on a low warning. "But I could always tell you more. For a price... of course."

"And what of that price?"

This time when his eyes land on me, they remain. I swallow hard and he notices.

"I want you to do me a favor," he states categorically, now completely ignoring my sister.

"I am the one making the deal," Tatiana snaps, but his eyes don't waver from mine.

"What do you want?" I square my shoulders and feign confidence I totally do not feel at this present time.

"There is someone your Angel of Death wishes to take. I, however, want him to stay alive a touch longer."

"I have no power over the Angel of Death."

"Oh, but you do." He raises his brows knowingly. "You get your Angel of Death to keep my breather alive and you have your deal."

"And then?"

"And then I will answer anything your heart desires."

"It can't happen that way," Tatiana interjects. "We're not coming back here again, it's too risky."

"You don't have to come back. You can call on me, and I'll be there." He turns his attention back to me.

"Wings, what do you say?" *Wings?* Now he has taken to calling me Wings? His eyes are alight with humor, and I am at a loss for words. I look to Tatiana and she nods her head.

"I can't guarantee that I will be able to summon the Angel of Death to pass on the message. He comes to me, not the other way around," I say, stepping on the barrier.

"Don't make the mistake of thinking he isn't always watching you." His words are salacious, but I ignore his jibe. "Find him, Wings. And when you complete my request, summon me once more." His fingers graze my cheek. They're hot and burn at the touch. "Tick, tock, Wings."

The demon winks before he vanishes as quickly as he came. The overwhelming smell of sulfur lingers in his wake. Surrounding us, the wolves' chests are heaving, their desire to shift close to the breaking point. My own breathing is heavy and jagged as I absorb the request.

I just made a deal with a demon, and that always comes at a price. I have either made a smart move that will keep us all safe, or I have just committed the most foolish of mistakes.

Chapter Nine

"No, no, what they say is never the truth. They mix that truth to get what they want. We can't trust that he will," John says, stepping in.

Tatiana shakes her head.

John goes to speak but whips his head around fast, smelling the air. "Run, *run!*" he screams.

We don't need to be told twice. Our legs go fast. Tatiana and I try our hardest to keep up with the wolves, but it's impossible, they are too quick on their feet.

When we get close to the next ward, I hear a hiss, then I am thrown backward, my back slamming into the ground, the wind knocked right out of me. I hear Tatiana scream, then see lightning crack above me, and I know she is using her powers. As I try to sit up, someone is on me, pinning my hands to my sides, his body putting pressure on mine.

"Little witch, why do you smell so good?" he sneers above me. I try to shake him off, but it's no use, he is stronger than me. I am no match for a vampire, especially the older ones—they are stronger and faster than the younger ones. If I had a wooden stick and he was young, I could attempt to fight him off. But I know he isn't new, because vampires aren't allowed to populate. It's forbidden. And if he were new, he would already be biting my neck.

"You are going to taste like sunshine, I can tell." His mouth comes down and his fangs pop from his gums. If he weren't a soul-sucking leech, I would say he is attractive. Most are, with their perfect skin and toned bodies. Just as I feel his fangs touch my neck, he is off of me. My eyes are closed, so when I open them, I see Grim standing above me, shaking his head.

"Demons and vampires? Really, little fighter?"

It still amazes me how everything stops when he is here.

I stand, shaking the vampire off me, but it still feels as if he is on my skin, tainting it. When I look over, Tatiana's eyes are wide and frozen. *Does he have a pause button?*

"What can I say, my life is complicated right now."

He shakes his head, his dark hair fanning around

his eyes. Grim has always been the untouchable yet incredibly attractive man in my life. And because he is in my life when I least expect him to be, I don't get nervous around him, even if he is the most beautiful man I have ever seen.

"I won't take the man he asks of, only this once, little fighter. Don't expect it again, though. This will be a one-time deal."

"Thank you," I say, and I mean it. What surprises me is I didn't even have to ask him about the deal.

He nods his head and looks around, then comes back to me. "I take it I can't remove you from here?"

I look around too, checking over everyone.

My sister is here.

I won't leave her so my answer is simple. "No."

"Figured. Use your powers." I nod my head, and everything becomes live again.

Tatiana continues to run to me, then a frazzled look crosses over her face. I was lying down a mere second ago with a vampire ready to gnaw on my neck, and now I am standing right in front of her. She doesn't have time to ask any questions as she grabs my hand and starts to pull me, trying to get past the ward without being bitten. Once they bite us, they won't stop—our blood to them is their own aphrodisiac. She gets to the border with me by her side, but as she goes to climb through—to get to where John is reaching for her—a hand tugs on me.

This time, though, I don't fall to the ground.

My powers are ready.

I turn to him, seeing that his lips are sneered up, his fangs ready to bite, so I shoot whatever is in my hand at his chest. It goes straight to his heart, and in an instant, he is dust. It shocks me so much that I stand there staring in awe from the dust to my hand.

"Move, Talia!" Tatiana's voice screams, and somehow, it gets through to me. That's when I see two more running at me, and I know they can reach me if I don't move now. I am just about through when something grabs my foot. Tatiana notices straight away and pulls me hard, yanking me all the way, landing on her. "Gosh," she says with her eyes closed, sprawled beneath me.

"Grim said he would do as the demon asked, so we have to call the demon back." Her eyes spring open, and I push off her to stand. She does the same.

"What?" She waves her hands around. "I don't understand. Are you a telepath now, Talia?" I shake my head and look back. I want to move. If we can get through that ward, why can't they? I start walking and so does everyone else, and it's then I realize we are down two werewolves. I look to John and Patrick, both of them have their heads down. Desolation etched on their faces.

Shit.

I stop and so does Tatiana.

"I'm sorry."

John nods his head and continues walking. Tatiana looks over, and I can see her fighting with herself. She makes a decision and runs to catch up to him. Patrick walks next to me.

"I didn't even notice till just now."

"They knew the risk going in," Patrick states.

"You're bleeding." His arm is gushing blood, it's running down his skin and dripping off his hand. He looks at the wound, then back to the road, not caring. "It will heal."

I drop to the ground and grab some herbs from the base of the trees. Catching up, I stop in front of him. His brown eyes lock on me, and after creating a poultice, I reach up, placing some in his wound to stop the bleeding. He nods his head in thanks, and we continue to walk.

"I felt it when everything stopped."

I look ahead to see Tatiana with her hand on John's arm. "You did?"

He nods his head. "How come you don't pause like the rest of us?"

That's a good question and it's something I've

never thought about until right now. "Maybe because he is seeking me when he comes?"

He shakes his head. "I've been around a long time, and I know no other angels can stop time apart from the Angel of Death." I did know that. But I am not one to share any details about Death. I like that we have our very own bubble that no one can crack. Even if I don't know everything I want to know about him.

"I don't know, then."

"Who were your parents?"

"Witches. They died when we were young, though. Tatiana basically raised us." Our father, we don't have much memory of him, and our mother never spoke of him. But not long after he passed away, so did she, just a few years later. Sickness.

"Time wouldn't stop for your sisters if you have the same blood. I wonder why it stops for them and not you." Patrick huffs, not able to make sense of this, and making me question everything right along with him.

"Again, I don't really know. My only answer is because I'm the person he is here to see."

"He seems to have an interest in helping you. Death doesn't negotiate. He simply takes," Patrick says as he keeps walking.

I stop, wondering why that would be.

* * *

"It's their fault!" one of the wolves screams at John, and he shakes his head at her.

"He chose to come, knowing the risks, Patrice."

Patrice is angry, rightfully so. It was her mate who died. I didn't even learn his name, yet this man died for reasons I am still trying to work out. I don't even know what's really going on. I haven't had time to process. First, I was shopping. Then, I was being dragged to the queen. Then the werewolves, and now vampires. How much more is there to come? My life was so quiet, and now it's rapid-fire and dangerous.

"I don't care. We are not going to die for the witches," Patrice declares and a round of applause follows.

I drop my head, feeling ashamed.

I shouldn't have come here.

A loud growl follows, and we all turn to John. His eyes are flashing, and the werewolves' heads all bow in response. I look to Tatiana, wondering if we should be doing that as well, and she rolls her eyes. I can't help the laugh that follows, making every head swing to me.

"They mock us!" one yells.

I cover my mouth and Tatiana stands. "We don't mock you. Now shut the fuck up. We aren't expecting anything from you. Just a place to stay," Tatiana snaps.

"You aren't expecting anything from us? Really?

You come here and take our alpha like he's yours to begin with. He follows you around like you're his mate, and then you take our men into the vampire ward. Yeah, sure, you don't expect anything," the wolf scoffs at her. I shake my head and step away, going to Patrick. I walk into the house next to John's and find him at his table drinking whiskey. He looks up when I enter, raises his glass, then drinks again.

"How's the injury?" I ask, sitting down at his table.

He looks and smiles. "I shifted, so it's all healed."

I nod my head and look around because I don't know what else to say, but I don't want to be out there anymore either.

"They'll calm down," he says, nodding his head in the direction of the gathering outside.

"Can't really blame them for being angry. I did kind of just fall into your territory without warning."

"Technically, you fell on me."

I nod my head, smiling at him. "I did."

"So, you and the Angel of Death, eh?"

I'm not sure what he's asking..

"Come, Talia, we need to go into the woods to call the demon," Tatiana says while walking into the room. Both Patrick and I turn to look at her.

"The woods?" I ask, remembering those strange voices that spoke to us earlier. I don't want to be anywhere near them.

"Yes, we need to go. Come on, we've wasted enough time as it is." She leaves as she's speaking, clearly expecting me to heed her direction without question. I look to Patrick, who offers me a shot. I want to take it, but I can't. I shake my head and follow her outside instead.

I hear Patrick behind me and turn to face him. "You should stay. You don't have to come," I tell him. The fewer people I put in danger now, the better.

"Don't be silly. Let's go." He walks past me, slipping on his jacket as he goes, and I manage to take a deep breath and follow him out.

As we walk past all the wolves who are still arguing, I try not to look their way. But I can hear their vicious words.

John walks up to us, looking back to Patrick and myself before he stepping right up next to Tatiana. She side-eyes him but doesn't speak. It's as if she knows it's a losing argument. He doesn't plan to leave her alone at all. I smile at them as we walk deeper into the woods, away from the other wolves. The last thing we need is to make the wolves even angrier by summoning in a demon right in front of them. That would surely make them hate us more.

The moon is high, and the sky is dark blue when Tatiana stops and looks at me.

"Umm, so how do we summon him?" I ask.

"Say his name. He said you had to call out to him."

I nod. "So, what was his name?" I ask.

She tries to fight her smirk by shaking her head. "Valefar!" she screams. "Valefar," she says again. When nothing happens, she crosses her arms over her chest. "Valefar is considered a god among thieves. He tempts people to steal," she explains.

"How did he grant the queen anything, then?"

"Oh, that's because the little thing caught me in a trap," a voice snaps back from behind us. We all turn to the well-dressed demon standing there, looking rather dashing.

He looks at Tatiana. "Your voice is considerably annoying." He tsks at her, then turns to me. "He agreed?"

I nod.

"Good. Now, I grant you two questions. Use them wisely."

I look to Tatiana and go to speak, but she says my name quickly.

"Do not ask him a thing," she says. "It will be considered a question even if it's not one."

"Clever little witch," Valefar praises.

"Why?" I ask, Tatiana. She groans, and it's not her who answers. It's Valefar.

"Because we like to trick people into getting what *we* want. And I always get what *I* want, Wings."

I'm about to ask him why he calls me that before a hand wraps around my mouth, stopping me from speaking.

"What deal did you make with the queen?" Tatiana asks as Patrick releases his hand from my mouth.

"She is needy, that one. She wants power. So much power, I could only give her a fraction of what she wants. She needs someone even more powerful than me to reach for what she desires most," he says, his lip curling. "I'm going to give you this one for free." He winks at me. "She got the power, but someone else made her a queen," he says. The second it leaves his mouth, he is gone.

Chapter Ten

"Do you know who?" I ask Tatiana as she starts walking back toward where the wolves are located.

"No idea," she replies.

There are many demons, but not many interact with us up here. Valefar has a reputation of swindling those for more than they bargain for. "But it has to be someone more powerful than Valefar, and I don't think it will be easy to figure out who that someone is."

"The vampires might know," John says, making us stop mid-step. We both turn to look at him. "She has them on her side, so they probably do know. Well, at least their sire would."

"We can't just walk into the vampire ward and ask them. We have a bounty on our heads now, and the last thing they would do is help us," Tatiana argues with him.

"But *she*..." John nods to me, "...may be able to. Look, you're powerful, and you have a bonus on your side that none of us have..." He pauses. "Death."

I cringe before I tell him, "He doesn't always come."

"When hasn't he come when you needed him?" Tatiana asks.

"When I was sixteen, and I got attacked by that vampire," I remind her. I shudder at the recalled memory...

I was walking home from one of my trips to the market, and on my way back I took a detour. I shouldn't have. I knew better. But I wanted to, and when I did, I found a vampire in our ward who was smoking a cigarette. He eyed me, and he was much faster than me. He got to me, and before I could stop him, his fangs sank into my arm, tearing at my flesh. I screamed, and then all the lessons Tatiana had taught me kicked in. I used a spell to get him off of me. It knocked him out, and he collapsed onto the ground, then I ran. And never looked back.

. . .

"He didn't come then?" she asks.

I shake my head. "And you know how bad I was after that." I didn't leave my bed for days. I had no energy and everything in me was gone. It didn't just scare me, it did something else to me as well. Made me see the world differently.

"Yes, okay. So, you don't know when he comes," Tatiana remarks.

"No, I never have."

"Right! So, we can't bank on him. But we need to work out a way to get Tanya back. We don't know what the queen is doing to her, and Tanya isn't as strong as us." Tatiana looks down. "She's softer, more caring..."

I nod. I get it, I do. She's older than me and has way more training, but somehow, I can take her down in minutes and it shouldn't be that easy.

"You can try to break into the castle, but it won't be easy," John says.

"Crystal Castle is impossible to get into without the queen knowing," Patrick declares. We all turn to look at him. "You've heard the stories, right? About wolves turning to ash on the spot. She has some strong magic runes protecting it."

When the queen first came to power, the wolves tried to rebel, and in return, most died attempting to dethrone her. Some witches as well, since the wolves and witches have been allies for a long time. Not long after, the wards were created, and the only time the wards are all open at any one time is when we shop at the quadrant. We aren't meant to socialize with anyone other than our own breed. The queen doesn't want us together at any time. The witches and wolves combined seem to be too strong a foe for her. Even though she is a witch herself.

"Unless you have an angel."

We all stop at that voice.

Very slowly, I turn around, my sister already gripping my hand in hers.

"You aren't welcome here, angel," John hisses.

I tighten my hand on Tatiana, knowing full well it's not Grim. Looking up, I see the angel, Bronik, staring at me and smiling. He looks me up and down, then turns his eyes to Tatiana. A growl comes from John, which only makes the angel smirk at his indignation. This makes John angrier, and he steps forward, putting himself in front of Tatiana.

"I could have your witch, wolf," Bronik states categorically and without reservation.

It happens fast.

John shifts.

Then in one swift leap launches himself at Bronik, who does nothing but smirk, then side-steps, pushing him as he does so John lands in a crumped mess on the ground. Patrick starts to shift too, then howls are heard all around us. I shiver at the sound and push myself closer to my sister who is busy staring at John, willing him to get up. Eventually, he pulls himself up from the ground. His white fur with a black stripe down the middle is ruffled. Tatiana goes to step forward, but I pull her back. When she spins around, her eyebrows are pinched together, as more howls seem to be coming ever closer.

Bronik turns his stare on us as Patrick finishes shifting. When Patrick moves toward the angel, Bronik pulls the same move he used on John. But Patrick seems to be ready, after watching John fall, and stops. His claws, all black, reach out and barely manage to swipe at the angel's white shirt, tearing it. Bronik glances down and then back to Patrick with another smirk on his face. Then, in two seconds, as if everything goes in slow motion, he leans forward and slaps his hands together in front of Patrick's face, and I watch in horror as he drops to the ground...

...in what I hope is *not* death.

"What did you do?" Tatiana lets go of my hand, and in an instant, her hands are in the ground. She draws the energy from the earth, making her eyes go fully green as she stares up at Bronik who watches on with an amused expression.

John, who is behind Bronik, is now standing and moves two steps before he is frozen in place by a click of Bronik's fingers. I go to touch Tatiana, but she is so lost in whatever she is conjuring that I do nothing. The ground starts to shake around Bronik and then vines shoot up from the earth, enclosing around his legs and trapping him to the ground. He tries to move and looks down at Tatiana with a condescending shake of his head before he does the same thing with his hands, putting her to sleep.

Now, it's just the two of us.

He kicks the vines away now that Tatiana is no longer awake to hold them in position. One step out of the mess of vines and he is standing near me, his silver eyes fixed on me. "Now that *that* matter is resolved," he says in a deep, gravelly voice. More howls are heard nearby, and I can hear the footsteps coming closer. "We need to talk."

I look to John, then Patrick, and lastly my sister who is right near me.

"You don't plan to knock me out as well?" I ask.

"I have a strong feeling that it probably won't work on you." I give him a curious stare. "And they escalated that... I have no intentions to cause anyone harm." I look again to my sister when his voice rings, bringing my attention back to him. "They attacked me. What else was I meant to do?"

"Wake her up," I say, pointing to my sister.

Bronik scratches his chin, then nods his head. I watch as he leans down and touches Tatiana's forehead, his fingers swiping over it before he stands. Tatiana starts to move, and I drop down to grip her hand.

"You need to stay calm... he wants to talk."

Tatiana seems to know what I'm saying and instantly pulls back. "Angels don't talk, they do the queen's bidding," she sneers and wipes her hands on her black pants as she stands.

"This is true," Bronik speaks.

Tatiana walks past him and goes straight to John, stroking his long, smooth fur. "You mean us no harm?" Tatiana asks him.

"Not on this day."

"Wake him, then, before every wolf comes this way."

Bronik looks at me, and I say nothing, but he seems to be waiting for me to agree. I nod slowly. He turns back to Tatiana and John, then bends down, careful not to get his white clothing in the dirt, and touches John's forehead lightly with one finger. John wakes, and somehow Tatiana calms him straight away with a simple look, then he shifts back into human form, leaving him completely naked.

"You need to call the wolves off," Tatiana says.

John seems to remember why he's on the ground and turns to look where Bronik is standing and sneers at him.

"Mind your manners, wolf, or you will go night-night again," Bronik says.

I can't help rolling my eyes at him and step forward to Patrick. Leaning down, I check for his pulse, and when I feel it beating strongly through his fur, I stand back up and order, "Wake him up, too."

"This will get us nowhere. I came to talk, and they attacked. This isn't a game of cat and mouse," Bronik grumbles.

I place my hand on my hip. "Wake. Him. Up."

Bronik steps forward and is now directly in front of me. He isn't like Grim. Grim smells comforting, like you're standing next to an ocean when it's about to storm. Bronik smells clean like disinfectant. I don't know how to describe it other than that.

"You sure, witch?" he asks.

"Yes," I answer succinctly.

He nods and leans down, touching Patrick, waking him up the same way he did before. Patrick starts to move again.

Bronik stares at me, his silver eyes penetrating me, before he steps back. "How old are you?" he asks me.

"Twenty-three," I answer.

He looks past me to my sister. "And how old are you?"

"Twenty-nine," Tatiana answers.

"So, that makes the shy one twenty-six?" he asks, to which I nod. "Interesting," is all he says.

"Why are you here?" Patrick asks as he pulls himself up to a standing position. He is also naked, and I feel like today all I am seeing are penises. So much so, I look away, but not before noticing once again how both men are in incredibly good shape.

"I want the queen's hold to be broken. One woman shouldn't hold that much power," Bronik replies.

"You've served her for years, so why now?" I ask, confusion etched into my forehead.

"Because before... there wasn't *you*," he says, and goose bumps tickle my skin just at his simple words. "You are the witch in the prophecy, correct?"

I say nothing.

"'With as much destruction it will bring, it will also give us hope. Her reign will be no more.'" He repeats the words from the prophecy. It's not the whole thing, but certainly some of it.

"I'm not the prophet."

"You really do suck at lying," Bronik says.

John and Patrick have managed to pull their torn

pants on, and they come to stand near me. My sister is back at my side as well.

Bronik turns to Tatiana. "You've done a good job of protecting her," he praises. She doesn't blush at his words or say anything back. "But she is of age now, and you can't keep her hidden forever."

"You have the wrong person," Tatiana says.

I didn't know of the prophecy until I was eighteen, and I sure as shit didn't think it was about me. That was until one night when I didn't come home. I was twenty and wanted to sneak off with the other witches, but they didn't want me around them. They put their spells on me, tested me, but none of them worked. I was immune to their conjuring. And only one person could be immune to that.

The prophet.

Or so we had heard.

When I got home, I asked Tatiana. She shrugged it off until I asked her to hit me with a spell.

She knew then that I knew.

There was no going back.

Our mother had told her before her death and made her promise that she would do everything in her power to train and prepare us for when the day came. That when the queen found out who I was, she would want me dead. I was best kept hidden, but in plain sight was the wise choice.

It worked for years. My sister did as our mother had commanded. She trained and made me stronger. But we all knew the day would come when they would discover who I was. And with that knowledge, I would either die or the prophecy would be realized.

Tatiana was hoping for the latter.

Me, I wasn't entirely sure which option I wanted.

That's a lot of pressure for someone who has never been loved.

"You lie, but I understand why," Bronik responds to my sister and then turns back to me. "You have to get to the queen, but you cannot do that by walking straight into her castle. She will know and she will kill you the first chance she gets. You need to go around, and in doing so, you need to collect allies on your way."

"What?" I question, confusion swirling in my mind and probably written all over my face.

"You have to go through the Viper Forest. There you will find the Viper himself. He hasn't been seen or spoken to by anyone for over two hundred years. The queen has no say in that area. It's forbidden to go there, and anyone who does, does *not* come out alive."

"Then that's a death trap," John says, shaking his head.

Bronik turns. "It very well may be, but the Viper holds a special power that you will need to break the queen's barrier. And only he holds it. And if you want to save your sister, it's the only way."

"What power?" I ask.

"One where you break all the wards." He smiles, and my sister gasps. "Now you know why it is forbidden. You didn't think she would be given all this power without a failsafe, did you? Traps to undo it?"

"Why don't you get it, then?" Tatiana asks.

"I cannot collect power as Talia can. Am I right on that fact? That you can collect power?"

I look across at my sister, who closes her eyes softly, then reopens them. I can only do that if it's given. I cannot steal someone's power. Well, in all honesty, I have never tried to.

"And am I correct in guessing she can only get it if it's given?" Bronik asks, raising one eyebrow.

"Yes," I say.

Tatiana shoots me a death stare.

"Good. You must go. It takes days to get to him, and you must be on high alert the whole way. It's been named the Viper Forest for a reason," Bronik says.

"You could be sending us in there to our deaths, making the queen's job easier," Patrick alleges.

"This is true, but why would I do that? I could easily kill you all now." Bronik smirks.

"What happens when Talia gets through?" Tatiana asks.

"Such faith she will?" Bronik asks.

"Yes," Tatiana replies without hesitation.

"I will meet you on the other side." He looks at me, winks, then disappears into thin air.

"We aren't doing it," John states.

Tatiana walks past him and comes straight to me. "We need to change."

I nod and we walk back to the wolves.

We will do anything to get our sister back.

Any damn thing.

Chapter Eleven

We walk back with John and Patrick close behind us.

"You can't go. No one in history has gone into that forest and come out alive," John says more to Tatiana than to me.

"He's right, it's signing your own death warrant. And my guess is that's exactly what the queen wants," Patrick remarks.

"We have to, and you can't stop us. So please move so we can get our things and go."

"It gets frigidly cold at night in the forest," a woman says.

We turn to face an old woman who's barely standing. One eye is missing, and she stares at us with the only one that works. Her stoop reminds me of a witch from a fairy tale. If she had a wart on her nose, she would be perfectly cast.

"And you'll need more than what you're wearing. Lots more. Don't eat the food. Take your own. And remember, everything you see can and will deceive you."

"How do you know?" my sister asks.

The old lady simply smiles in answer before she walks off with her cane in hand and her old woolen dress fluttering around her ankles.

"Margaret doesn't know what she is talking about. She whispers about secrets that most think are false," Patrick assures while watching the old lady walk away. "But maybe she has seen more than anyone has given her credit for. Who knows? One thing I do know is, you are *not* going alone."

"We don't need you to come. We have done mostly everything alone. And you have your pack here. You can't simply get up and leave them." Patrick looks to John, who has his arms crossed over his chest.

"I can't leave," John says as his eyes fall to Tatiana. "And I ask that you don't leave either."

She scoffs at his words.

"That's not going to happen. Ever." She turns and walks inside to grab our things. She steps back out with two bags and a jacket, which she throws at me. "Put this on, we're leaving now."

I do as she says and pull on the jacket. When I turn to look at John, he's pulling at his hair, his skin bunching at the sides of his eyes in a pained stare.

"Patrick is going with you."

Patrick comes closer, his own bag thrown over his shoulder and he's wearing a jacket as well.

"Tatiana," John says her name, but she doesn't turn around. He stalks over, spins her to him, and grips her shoulders in his hands as he stares at her. "Don't die."

She simply nods. "It's not in my mission plan to die."

"Good, because I would hate to come after you. Not even death could stop me." She snorts at his words, and he leans in fast. Before Tatiana can stop him, his lips touch hers, and I watch with amusement as she goes still. She didn't expect him to kiss her, but when his hands move to her hair, sliding through it gently, and he tugs at the ends, holding her in place, she drops the bag and steps closer to him so their bodies are touching. I look away as they deepen the kiss.

Staring out at the dark, almost black, night sky, I know we have to go because it's now or never. We don't know what they're doing with Tanya. The queen has a reputation for being ruthless, and Tanya, well, her coping mechanisms are not good. The problem with

Tanya is that she's pure—probably one of the kindest and gentlest people you would know.

"I have to go," I hear Tatiana say.

"Just promise you will come back to me," John says. The pain is evident in his voice as he says it.

"I don't make promises," is all she replies as I feel her come up next to me. She faces me, and I have to contain the smile at seeing her lips all red and puffy from that kiss. "Don't say it," she whispers to me.

"Wasn't going to say a thing." Her emerald eyes hit me before she pulls her jacket on and starts to walk. Patrick says a few words to John before he comes up behind us, completing our group.

We walk in silence. The wolves have a large ward due to them needing to hunt and run. We walk for hours before we finally reach the border. It's weaker at the back, because most people don't want to cross here as it only leads to one area—the Viper Forest. And no one wants to go in there. Well, no one who is sane. And let's face it, no one has lived to tell the tale, so we have no idea of what's inside and how we will combat it.

Tatiana grabs my hand and starts chanting to break a hole in the ward. It ripples and a fine crack soon appears which creases and curls into a larger hole. Patrick is the first to go through, followed by me, then

Tatiana, and we turn back to watch the hole slowly close behind us.

"Have either of you been this far?" Patrick asks, looking around to the border before his kind eyes find us.

"No, never. We have never left our own ward," Tatiana states.

"Okay, well, let's hope we don't die." I laugh at his choice of words, and Tatiana simply looks ahead.

The forest is in front of us and it's beautiful. Green trees and flowers are showcased in every color—pink, blue, yellow, there are so many to choose from.

"Its beauty is deceiving, so I've been told," Patrick says. "It wants to lure you in to trap you. Once its deception is complete, then it will kill you."

"How do you know?"

"It's the stories... have you not heard of them?" Patrick asks.

I shrug. "Some, but I assumed they were just that, stories, to scare the kids into not entering." As we start toward it, Tatiana looks ahead, not saying a word, watching everything around her with cautious eyes.

"I'm sure some are, but I'm positive some are probably true. The stories have to come from somewhere, right?" Patrick says.

"Why are you here?" I ask. "You don't owe us anything. So, why are you here with us?" Tatiana slows her walk, and I know she wants to know the same thing. "It's our sister we are risking all this for."

Patrick pulls his bag up farther on his shoulder. "My mother used to tell me stories of the prophecy when I was a child, of when the last king ruled. He wasn't a bad king and we didn't have wards then. But we needed order, which he didn't know how to provide."

I remember the king—he was young, and he was murdered by the current queen, who was sleeping with him. Well, so the rumors say.

"Our people were dying, and the vampires were slowly taking over our towns. So, we put our faith in the witches. They are, after all, who the prophecy was meant to be about. But at that time it states 'her reign will be no more,' and we didn't have a queen, so no one really took it seriously. Until it was forced on us because..." he takes a deep breath as we step closer to the forest, and soon, there will be no going back, "...she died." He pauses, sucking in a breath.

"My mother, when the queen came into power, when she put up the wards and the witches and wolves fought back, she died. And before she left, she asked me to believe that one day, no matter what, I would do the right thing and help make this world a better place. She believed I would somehow help, and when you fell into my arms that day, I believed her. Because I knew right then and there you were special. Something about you screams it."

As he finishes his words, we remain silent. I glance to Tatiana, who's smiling. Tatiana has never let me believe I am better than anyone else. After all, we are all equals and fighting the good fight and keeping our heads down. Family above all else. If it came down to picking to save the world over Tanya, I would choose Tanya. There is no other love or stronger bond than family.

"You may very well die for your mother's beliefs," Tatiana says as we walk past the first tree. They are all lined up so straight, you can't see the next one after it unless you are out to the side. It's as if they have been planted that way and have been growing for centuries.

"Then I will die knowing I did the right thing." I cringe at his words. "And protecting my alpha's mate," he throws in.

Tatiana's head swings back and she eyes him. "I'm no one's mate."

"Yes, you are. And because you are, you are my alpha." He bows his head, and Tatiana's jaw locks tight.

"Maybe I'll kill you myself," she says, dropping down to a crouch and placing her hands in the soil. We wait for her as she buries her hands deep into the soft ground. Tatiana has strong powers when it comes to the earth—it's her strongest source to harness energy. She can read it better than anyone I have ever met.

"I don't get it," she says, pulling her hands out and wiping them on her black pants. "I just don't get it," she says it again, this time shaking her head as she stares at the forest floor.

"What?" I ask, stepping closer, and when my hand touches hers, I feel it too.

"It's all dead," she whispers.

Taking a deep breath, I drop my hand away from hers and look at the forest.

How can that be?

How can it look so alive, yet feel so dead?

"That makes no sense. We can see the flowers," Patrick says, stepping up to one of the trees and reaching down to pick a pink flower growing around the base. We all look at it, as confused as he is. When he drops it to the ground, it dies right in front of us, shriveling into nothing but an ugly representation of what was once gorgeous.

"Nothing you see is real. Remember that," Tatiana says. "Let's go. We need to get a head start and find somewhere safe to sleep."

"How long will it take?" I ask, stepping up behind her.

"Judging by the distance, it should take four days

to get to the other side that backs up to the Crystal Castle."

"Four days," I say, shaking my head.

We step into the tree line, and the power hits me straight away. It's like a force that smashes into you, but you are helpless to stop it. You are blind to it. I can feel it, but I can't see it anywhere. It weighs heavy on my chest, and I have to work hard to catch my breath as it assaults me with each step I take.

"Talia, are you okay?" Patrick comes up next to me.

"You can't feel that?" I ask. He lays a hand on my shoulder, and I'm instantly relieved at the slight pressure.

"Feel what?" Tatiana asks.

"It's like someone or something is pushing on my chest," I say, managing to stand tall. Patrick removes his hand, and the pressure isn't too bad now. I seem to have overcome the strength of it.

"Can you carry on? We can—" Tatiana turns back, and when she does, she stops talking. I spin around and all that's there are endless trees, seemingly going on for what looks like miles and covering the entirety of the space behind us. It's as if we didn't just step through, because no other side can be seen. It's as if we have been in here for days, when in reality, we have only just stepped inside the forest.

"What the fuck?" Patrick says while shaking his head.

"My thoughts exactly," I whisper.

"Okay, we need to go. Let's keep going straight." She starts moving and we follow. No movement is seen or heard. It's as if no one and nothing is here. It's quiet, so eerily quiet, all you can hear is each footstep you take and your heart beating in your ears. No birds chirping, no wind rustling the leaves on the trees. Nothing.

"Are there no animals in here?" I ask Patrick, who's looking everywhere as if he's afraid something is going to jump out at us at any moment. Which could happen, I suppose, if there were any signs of life, that is.

"I can't sense any, or hear any," Patrick says as we continue to walk.

"Let's just keep going, keep an eye out, and stay close together," Tatiana says.

We do as she instructs and keep walking through the trees—the trees that seem to never end, and look the same. It feels like we are walking through the same thing over and over again. I'm not even sure we're still going in a straight line.

Two hours pass quickly. We haven't slept in so long, though, and I'm tired. When I glance at Tatiana, I see her rubbing her eyes.

"We should rest."

"No, I'm fine. Let's keep going."

"You used power... you need to rest." As soon as the words leave my mouth, something cold hits us, as if we've stepped into a freezer.

"You all feel that, right?" Tatiana asks, looking around, her hands hugging her chest.

"It's ice," I say through chattering teeth.

Tatiana reaches into her bag and throws me a warmer jacket. I put it on at the same time she pulls on one of her own. "We should keep moving and see if it follows." They both agree and we start moving again. My black boots do a fraction of the job of keeping my toes warm. It's cold. So cold that the air leaving my mouth looks like I'm smoking.

"Just keep going. If we walked into it, we are sure to walk out of it," Patrick says. I step closer to Tatiana, reaching for her and sliding my arm through hers to keep warm. She smiles, but her lips are turning purple.

"We may have to stop soon and start a fire," Tatiana says, focusing ahead.

"It's too risky," Patrick replies.

"No, we have to. Otherwise, we may freeze to death." She stops and I do too, seeing that the forest seems to come to an end. Before us is a river, and beyond that are rocks, low and high with the running water in the middle. We step closer, and the river bursts into sound, as if it just appeared out of nothing.

"We can find somewhere there to rest. It's been hours of non-stop walking and we need to sleep." Just then, a loud noise is heard. It echoes through the forest, and before we can even look at where the noise comes from, something is behind me, claws digging into my shoulder, and I am lifted from the ground.

Tatiana drops her bag and reaches for my foot, stopping whatever it is that has me in its grasp from pulling me all the way up. I check and instantly wish I hadn't. Its face is staring back at me, and it's the ugliest thing I have ever seen. Large, sharp teeth with drool dripping from them, scaly, with snake-like skin. Claws the size of my feet dig into my shoulder, and I feel the blood dripping from my arm where it squeezes, maintaining its grip.

"Death..." it hisses.

How it manages to speak through those teeth is beyond me. Drool falls onto my clothes, and I reach up with my other hand trying to get myself loose, while Tatiana squeezes my leg, and Patrick joins in helping her, attempting to hold me down. But the bird, if it's even that, pulls me harder, lifting me more. Its claws dig in farther, the grip only getting tighter.

Tatiana starts a spell, but it falls from her mouth as if it's nothing but words.

Nothing happens.

"It's immune!" Tatiana screams up at me, everything is.

I reach for the claws again, digging my fingers into its feet and squeezing. It screams as I continue my assault. I try again, feeling my own nails cracking under the strain. Its skin is tough, the scales making it almost impossible to penetrate.

"Move." I hear its hisses but can't look down. And I really have nowhere to move to. My feet are off the ground and the only thing keeping me where I am are my sister's hands wrapped around my foot. If she slips, just once, this thing will go. Its wings flap loudly above us, and it hisses once more as it finally lets go of my shoulder. I drop to the ground, landing half on my sister. I turn to look up but notice Patrick, who has shifted, is standing where I was.

"Are you okay?" I ask him, brushing off the dirt as I stand. He growls, and I watch as he pads over to us. His nose comes in close, and he sniffs, then rubs his mouth on us, letting us know he's friendly.

"It's probably warmer for him to stay in wolf form," Tatiana says.

Patrick growls in response.

I manage to straighten and help Tatiana to stand as well. She grabs Patrick's things that fell to the ground when he shifted. "We need to stay more alert. I didn't even see where that thing came from." Tatiana looks around dumbfoundedly. "There was no noise, no feeling, no nothing. I am always so vigilant. I'm sure there is more to come. We have to all be on high alert, watching for anything suspicious. Anything at all, because that thing got past my defenses so easily."

"Agreed, but we need shelter. We need to rest," I reply as Patrick nudges my shoulder. I cringe at the pain that shoots through it and the warm blood that I know is pooling inside my clothing.

"You're hurt, badly." Tatiana reaches inside my clothing, moving it away to check the wound. "Fuck, Talia. Fuck," she swears, and all I can do is smirk at her. "What?" She raises an eyebrow.

"You hardly ever used to swear, now it's like a second language."

"I always swore, I just didn't need to do it around you," she says, dropping to the ground and reaching into her bag to take out some ointments she made before the trip. It's still bitterly cold, and she tries to contain her teeth chattering, but it does no good.

Patrick, still in his wolf form, comes and stands next to us. I lean my good side on him, stealing his warmth as Tatiana applies her medicine.

"You are a pretty wolf, do you know that?" I say to Patrick as I touch his head, petting it. He stays where he is, leaning on me, taking all the attention he can get.

"Okay, we need to find a cave. Someplace to stay warm until the sun comes up," Tatiana says, standing and pulling two bags up onto her shoulders as she starts moving forward. My shoulder smarts, but I follow her anyway.

Chapter Twelve

Tatiana spots somewhere to crawl into right near the river. She ducks her head in as we wait, then she comes back out, nodding for us to follow her in.

Patrick stays near me the whole time as we enter, and when we step inside, Tatiana is laying the bags down, pulling out what clothes she can to throw over us.

"You think Tanya is okay?" I ask while sitting on the cold, dank ground.

Patrick lies down, putting his body right near mine. His fur is warm, and I run my fingers through it to heat up my hand.

"I think she's stronger than we give her credit for."

I nod. Tatiana lies back but I stay sitting up. My

shoulder hurts and I'm tired, but I'm not sure I can sleep.

"*Wings.*"

I squeak at the voice and look around but don't see anyone. The cave is dark, but that doesn't mean he isn't in here.

"*Wings, you lost in there?*" I know that voice, it's the demon we summoned.

How on earth is he speaking to me?

"No."

"*Tsk, tsk, tsk. You are a terrible liar.*" I turn to look at Tatiana and see her eyes are closed. Patrick's are as well.

"*You're hurt, Wings. Why don't you heal yourself?*"

"What do you want?"

"*Well, it seems Grim passed on our deal, which makes me not a very happy demon.*"

"I have no idea what you speak of. He said he would do as you asked."

"*I helped you, and I assumed you would hold up your end of the deal. But it seems you and the queen have that in common. You sure you aren't related to her?*"

"No. No, I am not..." I pause. "Who was it that you wanted to be saved?"

"*Oh, that's not your concern. I knew his time was coming. I was just hoping I could use him a little longer.*"

It's you I'm interested in. Where are you exactly, Wings? It seems I can't make physical contact."

"I don't think you need to know that."

"So, the stories are true. You are in the Viper Forest. Tell me, when do you think you will die? Tonight? Tomorrow? What a shame, he had such great plans for you."

Just as I am about to ask who, Grim appears. He looks down at my sleeping sister, then at me.

"You're hurt." He reaches for me, his hand gripping my arm as he checks my shoulder. "And you are talking to demons." He shakes his head.

"How did you know?"

"I can smell the sulfur." He crinkles his perfect nose. Grim is truly one of the most beautiful men I have ever seen. I will never get over that fact. His dark clothes show the outline of what I am guessing is an extraordinarily strong physique. I wonder when he works out. I glance at his hands, the only part of him I know well. He has strong hands, ones that send tingles all over my body when he touches me.

I quite enjoy his touches.

He drops to a squat in front of me, his face so close as he sits there. I reach out, and when I do, I flinch at the pain in my arm.

"Magic doesn't work in the forest," he says.

"So, how are you here?"

"Because I am beyond magic. I am death, little fighter. You be sure to remember that."

"Am I dying?" I ask, my fingers reaching up to touch his face. He smirks at my gentle caress, but little does he know I'm addicted to it.

"No, I'm not sure I am ready for that day. So do yourself a favor and try to get to the other side alive." He never pushes me away when I touch him. It's as if he craves it as much as I crave him to be around me.

"I'm going to heal you now." He brushes my shoulder, and I feel the burn as the skin starts to heal and grow back. Then I focus on him again.

"How can Patrick shift if there is no magic here?"

"Patrick isn't magic. It's in his genetics. It's how he was born." I glance at the sleeping wolf. "He likes you. I don't like him." I turn back and see him watching Patrick as I was.

"He saved me."

"And it's the only reason he is still alive." I laugh. "You trusted an angel," he says with curiosity. "Bronik wasn't always bad, but he now aligns himself with the queen. So, remember that next time you run off to do something he says."

"How do you know everything?"

He stands, my hands falling back to my sides as I look up at him.

"I'm always watching, little fighter. You are my favorite memory."

Then he's gone.

I look down, and my sister and Patrick never moved, they are both sleeping as if nothing happened. I scan the cave and don't see the demon either.

Resting my eyes, somehow, I fall asleep.

Now pain-free and more at ease.

I'm warm. I was cold when I went to sleep, but now I'm warm. Opening my eyes, Patrick is right next to me in wolf form. Tatiana is staring at me, and when I rub my eyes, I see she is focusing on my shoulder.

"It healed," she says.

"Grim." I give her the one-word answer she wants. "He also said no magic works in the Viper Forest."

"So, how do you explain that?" She nods to my shoulder.

"No one's magic but his."

"And he couldn't stay to give us a helping hand?" She scoffs. "What use is he, really?"

"He has his uses." My hand falls into Patrick's fur as Tatiana stands.

"The sun is out. We should be on our way. Three more days and we should reach the other side."

Patrick lifts his head and then stands.

"We don't know what else is out there, so carry this." Tatiana pulls out a knife from her backpack and I take Patrick's knife. "Do you want to train before we leave?" I look at the knife in my hand and nod. We put our bags down, and she steps back, stretching her neck, then moves her body so she's in a fighting stance.

"Right," she calls as she moves with her knife, heading toward me. I block her with my forearm, and she moves fast. "Left," she says, doing the same move just as fast, coming at me. I manage to block her again, and she smiles. "Feet." She drops down and kicks her leg out to knock mine out from under me as she spins. But I jump, avoiding her kick by mere inches. Tatiana stands and wipes at her brow. "You have gotten so good." She hasn't managed to get me down on the ground in a long time. Tatiana taught me how to fight, and she is one of the best I know. Not many could take her in one-on-one combat.

"Do you think mother would be proud?" I ask.

Our mother is the one who taught Tatiana how to fight. Tatiana had more of a connection to her than I did because she was older and understood more. To me, Tatiana raised me, and therefore, she is the one who taught me almost everything I know.

"I'm proud of you, so I know she would be."

We don't talk about her much, or her death—it was the sickness. And I don't really remember too much other than what my sisters tell me.

"I'm proud of you, too. I want you to know that," I say, stepping up and wrapping my arms around her neck. She hugs me back, both of us still clutching our knives. When we pull away, she slides her knife into her pants at the back, and I mirror her actions with mine.

"But we aren't complete without Tanya," Tatiana says, and I nod in agreement. Patrick slides in next to me as we make our way out of the cave.

When we reach the entrance, the sun is up and it's warm.

"Okay, this place is weird," I state categorically while looking around. "It feels so safe. So good." And it does, but I know it's all a lie. This place is death. Despair. Misery. Gloom. There is nothing good about this forest. Everything in it is either lifeless or inanimate. Nothing is as it seems.

Patrick starts to growl, his ears pointed forward as his lips form into a snarl. I follow his line of sight, and what I see has me standing stock still.

How is that possible?

I have heard of monsters in stories, but this? I don't even know how to describe this.

It's a group of women—four and counting—

standing on the other side of the river. They are on fire. Literally. Their faces are hard, almost scaly, the same as the bird thing that had its claws in me.

"You aren't welcome here." The one who has stepped forward, close to the riverbank, speaks. "And you will die like all the others who have threatened to come onto our land." Her hand raises, and on it she seems to form a fireball.

Tatiana's hand reaches for mine and she digs her nails in. "We mean you no harm," Tatiana tries to say, but they don't listen.

We turn when Patrick starts to growl louder, stepping in front of us and blocking our path. One of the women, if you can even call them that, throws the fireball toward Patrick. He manages to move, but not before it skims across his back, leaving his fur singed. He growls even louder, and I reach out to stop him from lunging forward.

The leader looks at us and smirks. "I never miss," she says through razor-sharp teeth.

"There is always a first for everything," I reply as Tatiana and I step forward so we are now standing next to Patrick. She throws again, and this time, she misses completely, which only angers her, making her step closer to us.

Tatiana and I have our knives in our hands which

we pulled out when we spotted the women, and I watch as Tatiana raises hers so fast that when she flings it, it hits the woman in the shoulder, making her scream out like some sort of banshee as the wall of fire that surrounds her extinguishes.

Gone is the appearance of scales and razor teeth. What now stands before me is one of the most beautiful women I have ever seen.

Her hair is violet, and it cascades in long locks down her back. All that covers her body is a small, white wrap-around cloth. Her full lips are pressed into a harsh line, and she looks at her shoulder, the lines between her brows deepening.

"How..." Tatiana says in shock.

I stare at the woman who's even angrier than before but no longer has fire covering her body.

"We mean you no harm," I say.

Her eyes, which are violet as well, lock onto me. "Harm," she says in a sing-song voice. It's almost like listening to music, which we rarely hear anymore. "You will die for this... slowly and in pieces."

Patrick growls next to me, and I reach for him with my free hand, trying to calm him down. But I can feel the anger emanating from his fur as I hold him tightly to my leg.

"Look, bitch, you came here to us. We didn't come

for you. You threaten us, and we will defend ourselves." My eyes go wide at Tatiana's words, so I squeeze her hand and she shrugs next to me. "What?" she whispers. "They started it."

I turn back to the woman as she pulls the knife from her shoulder and holds it out in front of her. "Witches!" Her lips lift. "It's been a while since I've tasted a witch." She goes to move toward us, but before she can, one of the women who is still burning brightly stops her by placing a hand on her shoulder.

"They are not yours to take." When she turns, her fire drops as well, and in its place is another beautiful woman.

"What are you?" The words leave my mouth before I can even stop them.

"You do not know? Is your world really lost?" the one who stopped the other asks.

Patrick growls and shakes his head. Then I feel him shifting, so I pull my hand away. All four ladies turn to him, none of them on fire any longer. They each stand there with beautiful violet hair and skin that's delicate and smooth, the scaliness of before now gone, and in their place the most breathtaking women I have ever seen. If they weren't moving, you would swear they are porcelain dolls.

We watch as Patrick shifts. It takes a while, but when he's back, he stands beside us very much naked.

"Our world isn't lost," Patrick says, then his warm eyes turn to face me. "She will save it."

The one with the injured shoulder sneers at Patrick's words.

"She is nothing but a witch. Her powers are useless here."

"What is your name?" I ask, and she rolls her eyes.

"Cinitta, but I only grant you my name because I know I will kill you."

"Cinitta..." I let it roll off my tongue. "I've read about you," I tell her. Her eyes go wide as I search my mind for that story. I know it, and her name was in the book. "Your mother was a fire witch, and your father a fairy. It's why you are able to change appearances." I recall the words in my mind. "She had four children... all girls. And because those species shouldn't have been mixed, because the fairies were all killed, your mother took you all to the Viper Forest and made a deal with the Viper King."

Cinitta stares at me, a mixture of shock and what looks to be sadness in her eyes.

"You dare speak of her." She comes toward me, her knife still in her hand. I flick my eyes to it, then back to her. Her long hair floats behind her like a waterfall as she moves faster until she is almost in front of me. Lifting the knife and taking aim, I remove my hand from my sister's and block her, hitting the arm that holds the knife. I push against her chest until she falls backward. It all happens so fast that when she stands and comes back at me a second time, she manages to cut my arm, just slightly, before my sister delivers a kick straight to her chest, knocking her to the ground on her ass.

"We didn't come here to harm you," I tell her again.

Patrick lifts my hand and inspects the cut.

"It's not deep."

"Sister."

Cinitta stands, her eyes furious as she looks at us.

"Sister."

Cinitta finally turns to look at her sisters.

"Let them be."

I can see the fire starting to gather around her now that the cut in her shoulder has healed.

"She drew blood from me."

"Let them be." The other sister touches her through her fire.

Cinitta turns back to us. "I should kill you, rip your head from your body for daring to speak of my mother." She takes a breath. "You don't let mention of her fall from your lips again."

They all turn in unison and we watch as they start to walk off.

Cinitta looks over her shoulder, staring right into my eyes before she speaks. "We will be watching, and when the opportunity strikes, there will be no prophecy anymore."

No one speaks until they are well out of sight.

Chapter Thirteen

We don't wait around after the four women leave. Patrick manages to dress in what we packed for him, before we are on our way again.

"I haven't seen anything like that before," Tatiana whispers as we walk. The forest is also unlike anything we have seen before. From the outside, it seems dark, dangerous, and once on the inside, its beauty will deceive you in ways that will kill you.

I wonder if the Viper has made it that way.

"What do we know of him, really?" I ask, looking between Patrick and my sister.

They exchange a glance before shrugging.

"Only what we are told as children. That this is the place you go to die, and no one has ever ventured in here and lived. Well, no one I have ever heard about," Patrick says.

"They were fire witches," Tatiana says, still musing about the four women.

"And fairies," Patrick finishes.

"How can that be?" Tatiana asks.

"I guess it will be the same when you and John have kids. Part wolf... part witch," Patrick says, which makes my sister stop and her eyes turn hard.

"I am *not* having kids. Bringing kids into this world is selfish and stupid," she spits.

"John is destined to have kids," Patrick says, completely indifferent, not noticing that we have stopped as he keeps walking.

"What?" my sister screeches.

Patrick jolts at her tone and looks back. "When he was younger, before the new world, a seer read him."

We give him a puzzled look.

Seers don't exist anymore. The queen had them all killed, along with many other gifted people. It's been over eleven years since she took the throne, and I struggle to remember what it was like before her. Granted, we needed order, but not her type of order—no way in hell.

"His heir is to rule the wolves, greater than he ever could, and that's saying something, since John is the best we have ever had."

"I'm not having any damn kids, so he better start fucking other people, because it won't be me."

My eyes go wide at her harsh words. "You really don't want kids?"

"No," she says, not even missing a breath.

"You would be a great mother."

"And the earth is slowly dying, and we are letting it. Why on God's green earth would I ever choose to bring someone into this world when I can't even protect my own sister?" She turns and catches up with Patrick, who starts walking with her. I follow as we go deeper into the forest.

"Tatiana..." I walk up behind her.

Suddenly, a gust of cold air hits us and we all freeze. It's not like your average wind, and not like anything we felt yesterday. No, this one is colder than I have ever felt before. I stand still and hug my arms to my body as the wind grows louder and the area fills with fog.

"Tatiana," I call again, not able to see her through any of the whiteout now surrounding me.

My brown hair whips across my face and hits my freezing lips. I kneel to cover my legs and hug them tighter to give myself as much warmth as I can, hoping this will go away soon. When my teeth start to chatter loudly, the fog vanishes, and in its place is rain. Heavy rain followed by hail. I look around, my hands touching the ground, searching for anywhere to hide my head so I don't get pelted to death, then start to crawl. My hands are covered in mud, and my knees are the same. I tell myself to move faster, but my body is locking up, ceasing due to the incredible chill that has overtaken me. My body wants to give up, curl into itself and find warmth. But, no, I keep moving until I reach a tree and place my numb, shaking hands on it. I know I'm at least half safe from the hail if I stay here, the branches of the large tree providing some shelter.

"Talia." My back straightens at the sound of my sister's voice, and my eyes frantically search for her.

How did everything change so quickly?

"Told you I would find you." A hand grips my shoulder and I'm pulled backward. I don't drop to the ground, though my body is dragged through the rain and hail as hot hands hold on to me and pull me away from where I know my sister is located. I scream and try to rid myself of her grip, but it's no use. I cannot move, and she's stronger in here—this is her home, after all.

"Cinitta," I say her name, but she sneers at me in return. Not letting me go as she moves farther from Tatiana and Patrick. The rain and hail stop, and the sky clears, as if the storm never happened. I'm about to say something, when I'm dropped to the forest floor and then sat on. I watch as she loses her scales and sits on my chest, pinning me to the ground. A sinister smile touches her lips as she stares down at me.

"You dare say my name, as if you have the privilege to do so." She leans forward, her face now inches from mine, her violet eyes shining bright as she pins me with her stare. "I usually like to end my kills fast and efficiently. But you..." Her hand lights up and fire coats her palm as she touches my shoulder just barely enough that the burn intensifies, and screams start leaving my mouth. "You think I will play with a prophecy? No one has ventured in here to help us. Those who come in here usually have no choice, or think some hidden treasure hides in here. They pay for their foolish mistakes with their lives, the same way you will."

Her hand comes back down onto me, with more force this time, and I scream again, but she only smiles as her violet hair falls around her shoulders. I buck and buck some more, causing her to move the barest bit. When she does, I do it again until she lifts ever so slightly, and I push at her, getting my hands free and then throwing her to the side until I'm on top of her. I pin her arms to her sides the same way she did mine, and she starts to buck immediately, but I know how to keep her still because my sister would do this to me often.

"If I were a madwoman, I would slice your throat,"

I say, leaning down. Her flames are gone and in their wake is a fiery glare. "But I think there is enough madness in this world. Now, tell me how I get back to my sister."

Cinitta starts to laugh, and I feel her belly rumble beneath me as she does. I watch her with caution, knowing full well she could light me up at any moment.

"The Viper will have you for breakfast. My death would be nicer... you should let me finish you. Kill you before you reach him, or shall I say, he reaches you. The rain and fog were just the start..."

"He did that?" I ask, confused.

"He controls everything. He knows you're coming now. And he will *not* let you reach him so easily."

"You've spoken to him?" I ask.

She smiles, her razor-sharp teeth wanting to strip my flesh from my bones, snapping at me.

"Viper likes his solitude. He invites no guests and requires no minions. He doesn't need any either unless he wants to."

I look down at her, still pinned to the ground by my body. "If I get up, will you tell me where my sister is?"

Her eyes go wide, like she doesn't believe my question.

"Will you?" I try again.

She turns her head to her left, then nods. I spin and spot a pathway, but that could be a trick—this forest seems to love them.

"That way?" I ask.

Cinitta nods, and I slowly and carefully remove myself from her and stand. She goes to make a move to stand as well, and I offer her my hand. Her brows pinch and she bats my hand away as she pushes herself up.

"You are a strange witch," she comments.

I turn back and see her eyeing me up and down.

"Should I take that as a compliment?"

Her violet hair flicks across her face, but she makes no move to shift it. "I despise witches. They look out for their own kind and do not agree with mixed breeding. It's the reason my mother had to bring us here to begin with."

"I don't agree with their views, and especially with the queen's," I add. She shouldn't be queen.

Her head cocks to the side. "Maybe I will *not* kill you after all."

"I think you tried that one already."

"You choose to be a smartass."

"I choose." I smile, and she doesn't know how to take it at first, her forehead crinkling as she looks away.

Her eyes fall back to me. "The Viper is watching you. You should be aware of that." Then she starts to walk off, leaving me stranded where she dragged me. My clothes are soaked and I'm freezing once again. I no longer have my bag and have no way of knowing for sure where to find my sister.

"Cinitta." She stops and glances back. "Will you take me to my sister?"

She smiles as her only response, then keeps walking.

Right before my eyes, the fog swallows her, and she's gone, leaving me wondering what the fuck I'm meant to do.

I t feels like it's been hours. I'm still freezing, wet, and now exhausted from this endless search. I went the way Cinitta indicated, and have found no trace of Patrick or Tatiana. I'm lost, in the Viper Forest. This is not the place you want to be lost in, let alone by yourself.

"*Wings.*" I freeze at that voice. What on earth does he want? "*No point ignoring me. It seems I may be your only friend right now. Am I right?*"

"Wrong," I say out loud.

"*You aren't dead yet. So it seems the odds may be in my favor after all.*"

"Will you shut up!" I scream. My legs keep carrying me on. To where... I still don't know.

"Wings, why don't you summon your Angel of Death? He could get you right out of there."

"No," I bite back.

"I'm sure they're dead by now. Come to me, I may be able to help you. Save the one sister who still lives."

"You are a real ass, you know that? What is it with everyone? Do you not have a heart?"

I hear his cackle run through my ears and down my spine.

"Wings, you know I am a demon. Hearts are for peasants who believe in the possibility of love. We do no such thing. It's how we have survived the longest. We don't fall for human foolishness, and neither should you, my queen."

I go to say something back, like why he would call me that, but then I see it—a flash of what seems to be fur. I run to it, and when I reach the point where I saw it, there is nothing there.

His laugh is even louder in my ears. I spin around. *Surely, they have to be here somewhere.*

"Tatiana." My voice is loud and clear, echoing back to me through the trees. I'm not sure what I'll do if I can't find her.

I can't lose her.

I will *not* accept losing her.

Pulling my arms closer to my body, I keep walking and ignoring the laugh that echoes through my head. How the hell do I get him out of it?

"I'm impossible to get rid of. You just have to learn to like me."

I ignore him. It's best not to feed the devil.

I walk farther until my legs are sore and the sun is down and I have to rest. My legs start to shake, and as I look around, I see no signs of life.

Will I die here?

Will the last conversation I had with my sister be about fighting?

I miss her already and it's not even been a full day. It's the longest I have ever spent away from her. Hugging my legs as I sit, I stay near the river and stare off into the water.

I will NOT die here.

This is *not* my destiny.

No matter how much my teeth chatter or how much my hands shake.

I will *not* die here.

Chapter Fourteen

"Talia."

I hear my name, but I'm too cold to move, too cold to even open my eyes. I can hear the river flowing from where I'm lying, when I feel a hand touching my shoulder. It's warm, unlike me. My teeth won't stop chattering, but my hands have stopped shaking now, seeing as I can't even feel them.

"Oh my gosh, Talia, you're freezing." Warm hands move me, and soon I'm surrounded by warmth. I close my eyes, and I'm not sure how long they stay closed for, but when I manage to reopen them, the sun is setting. Moving my hands between me, Tatiana is in front of me, while Patrick is behind me hugging my back. When I look at her, she smiles and tightens her grip on me.

"Did we lose time?" I ask her, worried.

"It doesn't matter. You're okay, that's all that matters. We didn't know what happened." She strokes my face, and I realize most of my clothes have been removed and all I am left with is my singlet and underwear.

That's awkward as fuck.

"I need to stand." Both move from where they have been lying and I get up as Tatiana hands me my pants, which I slide on, glad to see they aren't wet any longer. "I wish I could shower... a hot, steamy shower and not leave for hours."

"We're almost there. I think if we can walk most of the night, we'll make up our lost time."

I turn to look at Patrick—his eyes are downcast, his cheeks flushed.

"Thank you for doing that," I say to him, and that's when his warm eyes meet mine.

"Cold doesn't affect me as it does you."

I nod at his words and turn to my sister. "We don't even know if we're going the right way," I say to her, frustration building.

"You know the rules of the forest. It takes you the way it wants to. You don't get a choice. When the Viper wants to meet with us, it will be on his time and terms. Stories have said you need to survive a few days before he shows himself."

"Four days, the angel said," Patrick grumbles.

"How many days has it been?"

"Today is the third," my sister says grimly. "We need to get through today and hopefully... hopefully, he will show himself."

"He's probably watching us now," Patrick growls.

"He probably is. It is his forest after all," I say as we continue to walk.

So much of the forest looks exactly the same that it's hard to know if we are simply going in circles. We eat as we move, snacking on what we brought with us and trying to keep our energy levels up. Tatiana gives me another protein bar because I didn't eat last night. I eat it without complaint. The silence is deafening, so much so that all I want to do is somehow stop it.

Turning to my sister, I smile. "How about you tell us about your first kiss," I ask Tatiana. She ignores me and keeps on walking, looking straight ahead.

I turn to look at Patrick. "What about you? Who was your first kiss?"

His lip turns up at my words, but he does answer me and it makes me smile.

"My mate was the first woman to ever kiss me."

I try to hide my shock at his words because that means...

"She's dead, before you ask."

My smile drops from my face. "I'm sorry," I say,

and I mean it. I hear when a wolf loses their mate, their soul is never the same. It's split in two and it never fully recovers, as their mate is meant to be with them for life.

"It was a long time ago, I've learned to live..." Patrick pauses, as if he is lost in thought.

"My first kiss was to a warlock," Tatiana says, making both of us turn to look at her. "I was sixteen, and he was..." she pauses and looks up to the sky, "...dreamy."

"Aww." I smile at her words. I didn't know that. It's not something we talk about. Boys. Everything I have learned is from books, and that one time which was not a pleasant experience that I chose to forget.

"You kissed that awful boy, Malverick. I remember," my sister says to me, and I look away because what she doesn't know was that boy also took my virginity. "Talia," she says my name, trying to gain my attention. But I choose not to look at her. Instead, I keep walking by Patrick, who hasn't said a word since he mentioned his mate. "You've done more, haven't you." Her hand comes to my shoulder, and she pulls me around until I am facing her.

"He offered. I was eighteen and wanted to know more," I tell her with a shrug, pulling away from her touch and continuing to walk.

"How much more?"

I glance at Patrick, who seems to be back in this conversation and eyeing us both.

"Not answering that," I tell her, looking down at my feet. It's still fairly cold, but my shivering is not that bad anymore.

"Talia." She uses her best Mom voice on me, and it makes me halt where I am. "Did you have sex with him?" I see Patrick's eyes are wide as he looks between us, and when he spots me watching him, he turns away, rubbing the back of his neck, pretending not to listen.

"Yes," I answer with a huff, not bothering to lie.

"Oh my God, I am going to skin him alive, bury him beneath the ground, and let the worms eat him. Should have kept his dick in his pants."

"It wasn't like he made me. I asked, I wanted it," I say with hesitance, biting my lip. Because I'm afraid she will find him and do just that. "What about Tanya, she still a virgin?" she asks me.

"Yes, as far as I am aware, she is. You know Tanya, she's shy."

Tatiana nods and walks ahead of me, catching up to Patrick.

A loud swoop is heard overhead, and I duck, fearing that claws will be dug into me again, but it's not me it is after. It flies low and reaches for my sister instead. She rolls away, just missing the claws that would have dug into her shoulder, her face furious as she watches it turn back around to have a second go.

"I have a feeling we are close," Patrick states, looking around on alert.

"Why?"

He turns and points behind me. I spin around, and when I do, I wish I hadn't. That bird that tried to get me? Well, multiply that by ten and that's how many we see flying directly toward us.

"We need to hide. They have the advantage here," Tatiana says.

I nod, agreeing with her, and start searching around for something, anything that can help us. But there is absolutely nothing. We are in the open and no caves or trees are going to save us this time.

"It's quite interesting, don't you think?"

We all freeze at that deep voice. Can the birds talk? What is happening?

"That you three would survive when so many before you haven't. The last ones who survived in my forest were granted immunity to stay, and now they help me protect it." I turn to see a man, dark-skinned, with no hair and a smile that could light up the sky. But he isn't your average man, no, that you can tell straight away. His eyes, well, they are all white. He has on a robe that falls down to the earth, but it's not your everyday robe. This one is made of the forest—it's a rich, earthy green, and I can see the textured leaves woven through it. He wears a suit of velvet and the front of it is encrusted in what seems to be diamonds —it's as if he is wearing armor made out of the gems.

"You are Viper," Patrick says.

I didn't think Viper could see with his eyes being all white, but they fall to where Patrick is standing next to me. He closes his eyes and then something appears next to him. A woman, with long blonde hair, a small smile touching her lips as she looks down at her dress, which is pink with white flowers.

"Whitney!" Patrick says her name with such force that we all look at him. He starts stalking toward them, but Viper lifts his hand, and before he can take another step, greenery hugs Patrick's feet, holding him in position. "How?" Patrick cries, stuck in the same spot, unable to remove himself.

I reach out to touch his shoulder, to calm him, but he growls at my touch, so I pull it away. Then, Viper moves his hand again, and the woman who appears on the other side of him almost has me running.

"Mother," I whisper as Tatiana runs to her without thinking. She gets halfway before she too is wrapped in greenery and held in place.

Unable to move or even attempt to.

"Mother!" she screams. "Mother," she says again, this time her tone is one of disbelief.

Our mother looks at us and smiles—it warms my heart to see that once again.

Tatiana starts crying, and Patrick keeps on growling because he can't move.

When I look back up, Viper is standing there watching me.

"Everyone you would run to is alive," he says.

I don't understand his words.

"You have a very strong will." When he says this, he takes two steps and is in front of me. He reaches up, places a hand on my shoulder, and my head starts to spin as the forest appears to do the same thing. We, how do I even say it? Time travel? Because once we stop spinning, we are no longer in the forest, and my sister and Patrick are no longer with us. It's just Viper and me. He steps back, and when he does, he removes his coat, placing it over a seat made of nothing but wood before sitting down.

"I can see the interest," he says. "I can even feel it. You radiate an energy that matches even the most powerful." I say nothing. "And clever. That one would be thanks to your sister, I presume. The alpha's mate," he says, and my eyes go wide. "Would you like to know how they die?" He leans in to gauge my reaction. I can't give it to him. I came here to get something. I need to save my other sister. "Hmm... interesting." He claps his hands and out comes Cinitta. As soon as she steps out, her nose crinkles before she turns to Viper and looks down. "Yes, sir."

"Tell me... what should her fate be? Should she be executed like all others I bring in or should I allow her to live just long enough to..." He makes a snapping sound with his hands, making me twitch.

Cinitta seems to be uncomfortable, her hair not fiery, the violet locks flowing naturally down her back. She eyes me before she turns back to Viper. "That is up to you. She is at your mercy, sir."

"That she is. That will be all, Cinitta." She walks out the same door she entered. "Sit, let's eat." I don't want to mention that I haven't had a full meal in days or that I have no idea what the food that appears before me is. We live very simply in our house. We aren't part of the wealthy, and because of that our food is only a staple diet. I have heard of feasts before, reading about them in my books, but to actually see and smell one, well, that's a new experience, and as soon as I do, my stomach starts to make loud noises.

Turning, Viper has his hands in a prayer motion as he sits there watching me. But he isn't praying, he's simply holding them pressed together as he watches me.

"That queen is still being unreasonable, I see. Not much has changed." I don't understand what he's talking about, so I don't reply. "She has feasts like this daily, while you all eat rice. Does that make you mad?"

"She is the queen," I respond curtly, which should be enough of an answer.

"Not the rightful one, and she knows this. You, my dear girl, are going to shake up some empty graves, and I'm unsure if I want to watch that show play out or end it before it all begins." My heart rate picks up at his words. He smirks, knowing that it makes me uneasy. "Do you fear me?"

I lick my lips, the food smell now making my stomach upset. "Should I?"

"What an unusual answer," he comments, his white eyes roving over me like he's trying to find something. "And yes, you should. If you require your sister and wolf friend to live, that is." My hands clench underneath the table. "There it is... the heat in your green eyes. I've been wondering where it's been hiding, if it even existed. Thought you may be nothing but a doormat, but you may prove me wrong." He turns and lifts a miniature cake to his mouth, taking a bite, then nods at me. "Eat while I decide what it is I should do with you." I do as he says, biting into the first thing I grab. It's chocolate. My mouth waters. Oh my gosh, how I wish we had access to this at home. I've had chocolate one other time in my life, when I was around sixteen, and have never been able to get it again. It's expensive and we could never afford it.

When I look up, I find Viper watching me with intent.

"I could take you as my bride. You are beautiful." My breath hitches at his words. "And you are not a virgin. I do get lonely..."

"I..."

He waves me off, stopping me from speaking. "Sleep. And tomorrow I will decide your fate." He clicks his fingers, and before I can even argue with him, my eyes drop closed and I'm falling.

Chapter Fifteen

My hands are feeling something I'm unfamiliar with. What is that? Opening my eyes, I feel the bedsheets beneath my fingers, and it's the softest material I have ever felt.

"It's silk, in case you were wondering."

I sit quickly and see him shirtless, standing at the end of a bed.

Did I sleep here?

Am I in *his* room?

How did I even get here?

What am I even wearing?

Looking down, I'm dressed in something close to the same material I'm sleeping between. It's a night-dress with a slit up the side of my leg. Anger starts to rear its ugly head, and as I look up at him, he starts to speak, "One day, you will be strong enough to use those powers of yours in this forest, and I will not be able to stop you."

I take a deep breath. "Did we..."

He laughs, and I feel it's the first real emotion he has shown me since I got here.

"No. I may be a lot of things, but a rapist, I am not."

Letting go of the breath I was holding, I check around the room. It's nothing like my small box of a bedroom at home. This place would be fit for the queen's palace. Except everything is made of wood, with different earthy tones filling the space. Dark wood makes up the bed, yet the window bay is in a lighter wood. I sit up and slide my feet to the wooden floor, which is smooth beneath my soles, and turn to face him. He is watching me with interest, those white eyes studying me fervently.

"Your sister sure is a troublemaker." I wriggle my nose up at his words. "She is turning my forest over to find you. You must be special."

"Clearly, you don't have family," I snap back at him.

Looking around the room, my eyes search for my clothes but don't find them. My body is warm now, unlike how cold I felt in the forest.

"No, the family I did have was all killed many years

ago." I pause at his words and try not to look his way. "I can feel your emotions, Talia. No need to hide that face from me, too."

Turning now, I stand at the end of his bed. He slides his shirt on, and I watch as it glides over his smooth abs.

"How can you feel my emotions?" I ask.

"I know a lot of things. More than the average person." I stare at him, confused. "I'm the last of my kind, and the queen, with her black heart, would do absolutely anything to get rid of me. But you see, she can't. While she made deals with demons, so did I."

"Demons?" I ask, and he nods.

"We aren't all blessed with power like yours, but I was not going to let her win. Where do you think she got the idea to bargain with a demon in the first place? She knew I had," he finishes.

"You knew her?"

"Very much so. She was my lover," he admits.

Well, holy hell, I did not expect that answer.

"But you are..." I cringe at the word before I say it, "...old."

Viper starts laughing. "I may be older than you, sweet girl, but time means nothing." Viper is said to be older than most people but he never really ages. I didn't believe it until I saw him. He looks young, but his age has been hidden from most. We just know he is older than all of us, older than my parents, older than...

"Where is my sister?" I ask as I watch him go through a door that wasn't there a minute ago. When I follow, I walk into a bathroom. The floor is black, the walls are black, and the only thing that's white is the bathtub. Even the shower is black with a dark-frosted glass door.

"Shower, and when you are done, we can talk about your sister." I know I have to listen to him, that he has the upper hand here, but it isn't right. My hands start to clench and my eyes look around for something, anything, I can use to hurt him. "I would lose that thought. I know what you plan to do before you do it. If you want to see her, I would suggest that you *not* piss me off. Just listen."

"I bet all the girls listen to you and none tell you no."

His eyes snap to me, the whites so white that it makes you want to instantly look away. "Tell me... if I made you bleed right now, do you think your Angel of Death would save you?"

My heart rate picks up at his words.

"No. He cannot enter here until my time has come. So, you would be shit out of luck. Now, shower, you smell. And get changed." He walks out the door, and it closes behind him with a loud click. I would think I made him angry with how he just treated me, but I don't really know him all that well to judge him. There is a pile of black clothes sitting on the counter. They look remarkably similar to my clothes, but when I touch them, I can tell they aren't. This is real leather, where mine was imitation. The shirt is made from the same material as what I'm wearing now—silk. It's sleeveless and shows more of my cleavage than I would like. I reach for the jacket and stroke it—it's beautiful. Made of black leather with silver zippers all over it. I've always wanted one but have never been able to afford something this extravagant. I've seen a few vampires wear such a thing, but never a witch.

We don't get the luxury of clothes like this, unless you're the queen. She gets everything you could dream of, and more.

As I step into the shower, there are things in here that I've only seen in the markets for sale. Shampoos and conditioners in fancy bottles, soap that doesn't look like it's been used by everyone who lives there—this one comes in a squeeze jar. After washing my hair and my body, I get out and dress in the clothes he gave me. They fit like a glove. Perfect in every way.

As I go to leave, I search for the door, but there's no sign of it, so I step in the direction that he left and stand there. As I do, I hear a chuckle as the door opens.

I try to not look shocked. But as he isn't a witch, how is this place so... magical?

"I still want to kill you." Cinitta is standing there, her arms crossed over her chest defiantly as she glares at me with those violet eyes.

I don't move. I could probably take her in hand-to-hand combat, but in the forest, she has powers I do not possess. Her chances of beating me are more than double.

"But I won't. You amuse me." She turns and walks to the bedroom door, then turns back, throwing her hair over her shoulder. "Follow, witchy."

I do as she says and trail behind her out to a long hallway. The walls are gray and the flooring is white marble. My boots clink with each step I take until Cinitta stops at the door at the end and pulls it open. I peek through. There are a few people, and the sound of music playing drifts out to me. When I turn to look at Cinitta, she smiles.

"It's a party. Why are you standing here when you could be dancing in there?"

A party? I look back to where I came from and see no one.

"I would do what he says if you want to see your sister again," she whispers and basically floats into the party as if her words don't put me right on edge. I follow her into the room and the door closes behind me. I see Cinitta go to her sisters, and she stands there with a smile on her face, which is not something I have seen from her so far.

Looking around. There are humans, and is that...

I squint, and through the fog of the room I see a black throne, which Viper seems to be seated upon, with a drink in his hand as he watches everyone around the room. He notices and smiles at me. I do not return the smile. I don't want to be here. This is the last place I want to be, especially entertaining anyone. I want my sisters, I want us to go back to how things were, and I want nothing to do with anyone else.

"He beckons you." Cinitta is back at my side. I look past her to his throne and away again, my eyes taking in the people around me. "It's best not to keep him waiting."

I harrumph under my breath but make no move to leave. Instead, I try to discreetly scan the room for the exits but can't seem to find anything that resembles a door, let alone an escape route.

"Talia." The room goes silent, and all eyes fall on me. I see him moving from his throne and walking in my direction. "Since you chose not to entertain me, how about you watch as I entertain myself?" He speaks with authority, and at first, I don't understand his meaning. Then he lifts his hands, and before I know it, a cage appears. I turn to see him smirking, then his teeth show as he speaks. "I would watch closely."

I turn back, and before my eyes, my sister appears in the cage, followed by one of Cinitta's sisters. I quickly look for Cinitta, and when my eyes land on her, she doesn't appear shocked, but her hands give it away as they ball into fists. Her brows form a straight line as she watches her sister.

"Why?" I ask, barely breathing, not looking at him but knowing he can hear me. I attempt to step closer to the cage when his hand touches my arm, holding me back. When I face him, he squeezes his eyes shut, as if touching me hurts him. How could that be possible? A simple touch.

"Because entertainment is what the people want, so it's what they shall get." He removes his hand and claps.

It's then I realize my sister didn't see who was opposite her until now. Her brows pull together, and she glances around the room.

"She can't see you," Viper says with pleasure in his voice. "You could take her place." He says it so low that I almost miss it.

"I'll do it. Bring her out." Tatiana looks exhausted. Her hands are covered in mud, her hair looks like it hasn't been brushed for days, and she needs rest. But she's ready in her fighting stance, just as I knew she would be.

"Are you sure? One will not leave that cage until the other is dead."

"Bring her out."

"It shall be done." He claps and the room goes white. I blink a few times, and when my vision clears, it's me standing in the cage opposite one of Cinitta's sisters.

"Talia!" I hear my sister screaming my name, but I can't pay her any attention. My eyes zoom in on the woman with the violet hair. She looks puzzled until a voice comes through, then her back straightens.

"To the death," is all it says, and as the last word rings in the air, I watch as she turns into fire, scales covering her body, and she takes a tentative step in my direction.

What the hell have I done?

Shit.

I pull the leather jacket from my body and let it drop to the floor—it won't be of any assistance for this fight, as it doesn't give me free range in movement.

"She said he would play with you," Cinitta's sister says.

"What's your name?" I ask because I do want to know. She will be my first kill. The vampire I killed didn't have a soul so I do not count him, but her, I want to remember her name.

"You cannot defeat me, but because I know you will die, I shall give you my name. Araba, and I am sorry for your death," she says before she moves toward me. I watch her closely, though, her moves almost angel-like—fast and smooth. But even without my powers, I can tell when she's going to take her next step. She descends on me, and as she reaches for me with her fiery arm, which would be sure to scorch my skin, I duck and quickly elbow her in the ribs as I slide under her. She groans at the contact but turns fast to face me again. Anger now mars her face at the knowledge that I'm not going to be as easy a kill as she first thought I would be.

I turn to look behind me, for just a fraction of a second, to see if I can find my sister, but I can't see anyone, and that time cost me. Because before I can stop it, Araba strikes me hard in my stomach, then a hand goes to my face. I turn quickly at the sensation, and her fiery palm touches my skin, pulling a scream from my lungs as I fall backward. Her feet coming toward me are all I see as I try to drown out the pain with my mind.

I should be moving, screaming.

Fire! Fire sure is a sad way to die.

And painful.

Araba's hand reaches out to hit me in my face again, but this time I move, and she grazes the side of my cheek. It's like putting your hand over a flame for just a second. It burns, but it doesn't register straight away.

It gives me enough time to kick my legs out and trip her so she falls. I get up when she does and reach for my jacket, knowing I won't be able to touch her skin without causing myself pain. I quickly pull the jacket over my hands to cover them so I can punch her back. She stumbles but manages to grip on to my arm to stop her from falling. The pain of her touch is excruciating, but I can't stop to scream or pull her off, because if I do, she will have the upper hand, and I'm afraid of what will happen to me if she gets it.

She could very well kill me.

Taking a deep breath, I kick her with my boots, but her grip only tightens, then I do it again, this time making sure I get her ribs. When my foot connects, the fire drops from all over her body and in its place is a beautiful woman with violet hair. But I have learned they are just as dangerous without the fire as they are with it. Though, at least now my body isn't burning any longer.

"Tell her I'm sorry, that I love her. Okay?" Araba asks.

I nod and let her fall to the floor, then turn to face

where I know he was standing and look out to meet his gaze. Only he is visible as if he chooses. "You play a game of evil kings and queens, making us kill each other. You are both as bad as one another."

I feel her stand behind me and move in my direction. As she does, I step to the side, leaving my foot where it is so she trips as she runs at me, falling headfirst into the bars of the cage. The loud bang from her head hitting echoes all over the room, and when I look down, blood pools around her head.

A scream rips through the crowd, which I still cannot see but know is there, then the cage starts to shake.

"Araba!" Her name is screamed from a group of women who I can only presume to be her sisters.

"Is this what you wanted?" I yell into the nothingness, not being able to see a single soul again.

Then, before me on the other side of the cage, he appears.

Viper.

"Yes, it is exactly what I wanted. You had to know what it's like to kill because soon you will *not* have a choice. This was for you. Not for me, Talia."

"Lies," I spit at him.

"I knew you would take the place of your sister, and I knew exactly who would win."

A scream rips through the air again, and I know this one is Cinitta. I hope she didn't just hear her king play with her sister's life, knowing full well she was going to die.

"I want what I came for," I seethe.

He bows and the cage opens, letting me see the crowd gathered around. All eyes fall on me and scan me with fear. I look down at myself to see what they see. My clothing is singed and torn, and most of my skin on my body is now covered in red, swollen burns, my face probably no better off. When I glance to my left, Cinitta and her sisters climb into the cage and surround their fallen sister. My heart aches, and anger and disappointment that I was the one to do that takes hold in my belly.

To kill her.

I've never killed anyone with a soul.

Yes, I have harmed others with my powers, but never with my bare hands have I purposely set out to kill someone. My heart sinks as a hand grips mine, and I know straight away it's my sister without even looking, the feeling comforting.

"I'm sorry," is all she says. "But I'm glad you're alive." I feel her eyes inspecting me as my gaze stays glued to the cage. Dark blood coats the white floor as the sisters pick Araba up, her lifeless body hanging there.

"You're hurt, we need to tend to your wounds." My sister inspects me, but I pull my hand away.

"I don't deserve it," I say, knowing full well the pain I feel is what I deserve right now. What I have to suffer through. I need to know this pain because Araba can no longer feel anything. And that's thanks to me.

"Talia." His voice comes from in front of me, and as I go to open my mouth to scream at him and possibly even kill him, he touches my forehead and the world goes black.

Asshole.

Chapter Sixteen

As soon as my eyes open, I move off the bed and stand. My eyes search the room, and I find my sister sitting off to the side, her head hanging low, with her hands on either side of her neck. When she lifts her head, a small smile plays on her lips.

"You've been asleep for ages." I look out the window where the sun is starting to rise. I'm not in the same room I was the first time I awoke here. This one is all white and is the complete opposite of the other one.

"My..." I study my hands and arms and touch my face. The burns are all gone.

"He had a healer. She healed you while you were asleep," Tatiana answers my unspoken question.

"Where is Patrick?" I don't remember seeing him at all last night.

"Viper put him in a cage, said that's where the dog belongs." She stands and rubs her eyes.

"Have you slept?" She shakes her head. "Sleep, even if just for an hour." Her eyes fall to the bed. "I'll go and see what I can do about Patrick."

"I don't trust him," Tatiana whispers.

"And you shouldn't. Now, sleep. I'll wait for you to fall asleep before I go in search of Patrick."

She climbs onto the bed and turns to face me as she lies down. "I was so worried I had lost you."

"I'm here."

"I kind of went mad. I didn't listen to anything. Anyone who came near me, I had to get past to find you." I sit on the bed opposite her and touch her arm.

"Sleep. I'm fine. You are fine. Tanya is fine, too. We will all be together soon."

She closes her eyes and soon a soft snore follows. I wait a few minutes before I get up and leave the room, shutting the door behind me. As soon as I step out, Cinitta is there. Her eyes are red from all the tears she must have shed. My body goes into survival mode. But she makes no move to attack me, instead she looks deflated. Defeated. Broken.

"He wants to see you."

Do I ask her if she is okay?

Tell her that I'm sorry about what happened?

As I try to think of the right words, she heads off down the hall.

"Cinitta." She ignores me until we arrive in the same room where the party was held last night. I step up and go to touch her, but she pulls away and hisses at me. "I'm sorry."

"Come on in, Talia, we have much to discuss."

We don't.

I only have two things on my mind.

Give me the spell or potion to get through the witch's barrier.

And give me Patrick.

Viper cackles, obviously reading my thoughts as I step in. I briefly look back to Cinitta and I am filled with sorrow.

"Nothing you can do will comfort her. Unless you want to forfeit your life, that is."

Cinitta turns and walks off, her body lighting up in flames as she goes.

"She is deciding whether it's worth it to disobey me and kill you. You see... she likes you, but she loved her sister," Viper says from his seat at the head of a large table.

The room has changed since last night. In it now sits a massive dining table, big enough to fit more than ten grown men, but only he sits at it, right at the end in his damn throne.

He waves his hand to the food and smirks, knowing full well I'm hungry. "I see you have healed nicely."

"No thanks to you," I bite back.

"Hmmm..." His white eyes close for a brief second before they open. "It seems you still have no respect. Even after everything I have done."

"You haven't done any of the things I have asked you to do..." I pause. "You know why I am here, right?"

His elbows lean on the table, and his hands form together. "Right."

I shrug. "And have you supplied the thing I need?"

"The spell," he says, smiling. "You think I will just hand over the spell that will let you walk straight through her barrier, tearing it down? What if I told you a false one and sent you on your way? How would you know if it was true, that I didn't send you to sign your own death warrant?"

"Are you that type of man? One who lies and doesn't follow through on his word?"

He smiles, his brilliant white teeth showing. "I could be, if it serves me right."

And I believe him.

"But lucky for you, I do not wish to see you dead... yet. So, no, I will not give you a false one. But..." He smirks, and I know I won't like what is about to come out of his mouth, so I talk first.

"I've killed someone for your amusement, yet you still want more?"

His fingers tap together.

"Maybe you are just like the queen," I sneer.

"Can you guess what I am?" he asks. "If you guess right, I will let you, your friend, and your sister walk free. If you do not, the wolf is mine. He has so much hurt bundled up inside that it will be awesome to play with him."

My mouth goes to open, but he shakes his head.

"Think on it. Do you think you can risk getting this wrong?"

"I want to see him," I demand.

He eyes me and then simply nods his head once.

A door appears behind him.

"You have five minutes and then tell me what you think I am. So, think carefully." My feet move quickly through the door until I get to what looks like a bare, dark room. "Four minutes and forty seconds," Viper's voice rings out behind me. Ignoring him, I step farther into the room and look around. At first, I don't see anything until I check again. There he is in the corner, naked and scrunched down in a position of fear.

"Patrick." He doesn't move at the sound of my voice. "Patrick," I say again, this time a little softer. He moves fast and jumps, and when he does, he turns into his wolf, coming straight at me.

Then the world pauses.

Patrick is suspended mid-air, his wolf eyes set firmly on me.

"Little fighter." Grim stands in front of me, putting himself between Patrick and me. "He's a caged wolf. What do caged wolves do?"

"Attack," I reply, knowing this but not even thinking of it when I walked in the door. Grim steps past me and out to where Viper sits. I watch his body tense before he turns back to look at me.

I resist the urge to touch him, to have my hands on him and smell the scent that only I know he possesses.

How death could smell so inviting has me baffled.

"He's playing you. You know that, right?" Grim's silver eyes look to Viper. "I wouldn't stop you if you walked up behind him right now and slit his throat."

"So dark," I say to him. "I don't want to kill anyone else." I rub my hands on my pants, trying to rid that thought from my mind. Thinking about all that blood makes me sick.

"It would be the kinder thing to do, because his death will be painful."

"I will *not* do it."

He walks over to me, his hands grasping my hips, and he lifts me effortlessly before he positions me, so I am not in the way of Patrick's attack. "Will you not ask what he is?" Grim inquires, and I know he knows the answer I will need.

"I already know."

"That you do, little fighter. That you do. I shouldn't have expected any less, really." He nods and looks back at Patrick. "Be careful, there are only so many times I can save you."

"No, there isn't. And why don't you just let me die? It could be easier."

His cold hand reaches up and strokes my dark hair back behind my ear. "Because you are so much more fun alive," he whispers, and my eyes bounce open. I must have closed them at his touch. I love his touch— the things it makes me feel are beyond this world. Beyond any comprehension.

Death slays me, and I let him.

"Is my sister, Tanya..." I trail off, knowing he will know if she is alive or dead.

"She is alive," he answers quickly, and I take in a deep breath. "Your wolf should be calmer now." Before I can argue with him, he is gone and Patrick is moving full speed to the floor. When he connects with nothing but the hard ground, his head shakes and his eyes search around the room until he finds me standing there. His lip lifts to a snarl before his body shakes and he transforms back into human form.

"Patrick." I don't move. I don't know what will scare him, and it's best I keep calm around him. "We're going to get out of here."

He lifts his head to look at me and then lays it back down on the floor.

"I've been showing him visions of her." Viper's voice comes from behind me. "Reliving that pain, again and again." He smiles as if it's some kind of victory. "It would break any wolf. But this one, right here, is... he is strong. I can see why you brought him with you."

"I didn't bring him," I whisper, keeping my voice low.

"No. He chose his path."

"I guess you can see that, being a seer."

Viper laughs. "Among other things, my dear. But yes, a seer is what I was born as."

"Then you made a deal with a demon, much like the queen did," I finish.

"Indeed, I did. And unlike the queen, I got a better deal out of the transaction."

"Free him," I say, watching as Patrick curls into a ball.

"As you wish." Viper clicks his fingers, and I see the relief wash over Patrick's face before his eyes close and he falls asleep. "I think it's time we sit and eat, then you can leave." He turns and walks out the door. I follow, checking back on Patrick as an ease settles across his face.

What have I done to the people I love?

Who am I even?

"You, my dear, are extraordinary. It's why powerful beings gravitate toward you. It's why the Angel of Death saves you when he shouldn't..." He pauses. "He knows, though, when you will die, because like him, I also know your death. But he is saving you from a lot of pain and torment in the meantime. Must be nice to have an angel on your side." He murmurs the last part, and I am sure it's more for himself than for me to hear.

"You will give it to me, then?"

"I will, but I want you to know... this spell cannot be used by just anyone. Only someone with immense power can use it. It's why the angel told you about it. Your sister could do the spell, but it won't work, it would only end up killing her. Your queen was smart with her decisions on how to rule. She must have been planning these things for a long time."

Tatiana was friends with her at one point, and I wonder if she ever knew what was happening.

"The spell has to be chanted when the moon is at its highest, and a blood sacrifice must be made."

"What?" My voice squeaks at his words.

"Someone must die for you to work the spell. The blood you use has to come from someone you killed by your own hands. Then and only then can you say the spell and all barriers she has created will be broken."

Kill someone!

Again.

This is not something I'm willing to do. I cannot sacrifice an innocent, the blood will be on my hands if I do so.

"Even if the lives of everyone you love depends on it?" Viper asks, reading my thoughts. "There has to be a sacrifice. There is no other way. You cannot break magic this powerful without it. Surely your angel told you this?"

"No, he did not."

"I was only going to give you one of your companions to take with you, but now I am feeling generous, and I'll let you take both, so you have a choice on which one you will kill."

"I won't kill anyone again."

"You say that now, but Talia..." he leans forward before continuing, "...your destiny says otherwise. One day, *you* will be a warrior queen. Why do you think your sister has trained you so hard? She knows one day she will no longer be there for you, and you will only have yourself to depend on."

"You don't know me."

"But I do. I know you crave the touch from Death... or Grim, as you like to call him. I know you do not understand your feelings toward him. And soon, they will become even more tangled. You are going to be my favorite soap opera. In case you don't know what that is, it's what the humans used to watch for fun." He lifts his glass of wine and takes a drink.

"Sir." We turn to Cinitta.

"It's time." Viper stands, pushing his seat back. He walks over to me and leans down until his mouth is basically touching my ear, then he whispers the spell. When he pulls back, his face shows a blank expression. "You have two hours to reach the border. It takes three. Good luck."

I watch as he walks away and Patrick strides out of the room straight after he leaves.

"My head hurts."

I manage a somewhat weak smile and turn to Cinitta. She hands me a small bottle, and I take it, placing it in my jacket pocket, then follow her to where my sister is waking from her sleep. She appears rested.

"We have to leave."

"Take this." Cinitta hands Tatiana a small bag, then she disappears as quickly as she came.

"Shit! She can move fast," Tatiana states.

"We have the spell, and we only have a couple of hours to get to the barrier. But, Tatiana..." My sister is moving before I can finish my sentence. She doesn't know the consequences of what we are about to do, but I also have no idea how to stop her. My feet are unable to move as I watch her walk out of this place that has held us captive.

Patrick looks back at me in concern. "You are drenched in fear." He steps close and sniffs, using his perfect wolf nose.

"We can't do it," I tell him.

He eyes me suspiciously and looks over his shoulder at Tatiana, whistling to her. She stops and comes back to us.

"What are you doing?" She's flustered, I can tell by the way she is holding herself. Her eyes are flicking around, checking for problems. Her breathing is shallow but fast. She wants to leave here as much as I do, but she has no idea what leaving means.

"Your sister is worried," Patrick says, and Tatiana's eyes finally lock on me.

"Why? We need this to get Tanya back. Is that not what you want?"

"Of course it's what I want!" I scream at her, then instantly regret it. "There is a price to pay for breaking the damn barrier."

"And did you think it would be free? Not in all hell would it be free," my sister says while shaking her head. "You're smarter than this, Talia. Everything worth fighting for comes at a cost. Why are you being so stupid right now?" Tatiana only speaks to me like this when I have pushed her last nerve.

"He said the spell only works with a sacrifice..." neither of them speaks before I continue, "...and that only the blood of the person I kill by my own hands will work."

Tatiana starts walking again. "Hurry up! We have a ways to go and we can't be wasting any precious time." She ignores everything I have just said, but Patrick does not.

"We will figure something out. Come, before your sister kicks both our asses." He turns and follows Tatiana.

Taking a deep, centering breath, I take the first step to do the same.

Chapter Seventeen

We've been running. I'm tired and not even sure we will make it before the curfew. It takes three hours to get to the border in a forest we don't know, and we only have two hours granted to us. Tatiana doesn't stop, not even for one second. She is on a mission, and Patrick follows her lead, doing whatever she says.

We haven't uttered a word about what I told them. Soon one of us may very well die, and that fact saddens me, especially that it won't be me. I am the only one strong enough to open the barrier, to break it all down. I wish Tatiana were. I would offer myself up as a sacrifice to her so she could save our sister.

"Stop thinking and keep running!" my sister yells back to me without breaking her stride, then shouts to Patrick, "Are we close?"

"I can smell the lake," he utters.

She looks up. The moon is almost at its highest, the only time we have to do the spell. "Do not slow down." She swings back to look at me, and I nod, keeping up a good pace after her.

Running is something I have always been good at. I'm fast.

Part of me has no inclination to reach the barrier.

The other part is screaming in my mind to do everything possible to save Tanya.

She is nothing like Tatiana and me. She is soft, nice, and she has no hard edges, which are all qualities that worry me, considering where she is right now—with the evilest person alive. A queen who will do anything to stay in power.

Tatiana comes to a stop, placing her hand in front of her. I watch as the barrier shakes but does not move. This part is never guarded and no one is ever around here, because no one makes it through the Viper Forest, and who would want to escape into the Viper Forest anyway? It's a death sentence. I know for sure I never plan to come back. Ever.

"Angel," Tatiana hisses.

Bronik stands on the other side. "Witch," he says back to her before his eyes leave her and search for me. When they land on me, he inspects me from head to toe before they settle on my face. "You are well, then."

"Alive, yes," I tell him. "Not sure for how much longer, though."

"As soon as the barrier is down, she will use everything she has to put it back up. Everywhere."

"As long as we slip through and get what we need, I don't care what she does," Tatiana barks at him.

His silver eyes leave mine and fall to her. "You should be worried. Apart from your sister here, she also fears you greatly. And having the fear of a queen is never good." Bronik then asks, "You know the price of payment, then?"

"Blood."

He nods in confirmation at my words. "Not just any blood. Blood of someone killed by your hands." He repeats the words I already know.

"Yes, I am well aware. It would have been nice if you'd have told me that to begin with."

"Would you have left if I did?" His head drops to the side, studying me.

"Yes. She is my sister." I cross my hands over my chest.

"It seems you have some choosing to do. Your sister. Or the wolf."

"Neither," I reply. "I will not take either life, no sooner than I would take my own."

"There is always a price, Talia. There will always be a price. You have to remember to pay it."

Stepping back, I slide my hands in my pockets and shake my head.

Patrick stands in front of me, his head high. "I am choosing for you."

A tear leaves my eyes. "No. No way."

"I knew there was a reason I had to come with you. I just didn't know it was this. I'm ready to see my mate," he says, his mouth set in a sad smile.

"I could never..." I take a step back. Killing him is not something I can or ever will do.

"You have to, because it's not just her you will be saving, it will be everyone. It's for the greater good." My hands clench, and in my pocket, I grip the bottle Cinitta gave me, praying it will burst under the pressure, but the damn thing doesn't.

"It has to be done... and by *you*," Tatiana says. "If I could kill for you, I would."

My eyes, blurry with tears, search their faces before they land on Bronik, who shows no sign of any emotion. Has he ever, though, apart from confusion? I was told not to trust him, and a part of me doesn't. For all I know, the minute the barrier is down, he could step over and take me straight to his queen.

Hell, he could even kill me himself.

I have no guarantees.

Pulling my hand out from my pocket, I take the vial that was given to me by Cinitta.

Patrick eyes it and steps close until he takes it from my hands. "What is this?"

I shrug because I simply have no idea.

"Cinitta gave it to me before I left."

He opens the bottle and his eyes go wide in surprise. He looks to Tatiana, who appears as confused as I do, then to Bronik who says the words, "It's the blood of the dead girl... her sister."

Tatiana gasps at his words and Patrick nods his head, confirming. Relief floods through me that I don't have to kill anyone. And I owe Cinitta big time. Because somehow, she knew I woud need this.

"She can use that right?"

Bronik nods. "If she was killed by Talia's own hands, she can."

"It was an accident."

"But one you had a hand in," Patrick declares, forcing a shiver to go through my body. I had hoped not to be reminded about what happened back there in the cage.

"She could be tricking us. She could want me dead for what I did to her sister."

"This blood is not living," Bronik says.

"It could be a dead pig's blood for all I know," I argue.

"It is not," Bronik replies.

I turn to face him and scream, "You probably want

me dead, too. So shut the fuck up!"

He smirks at my outburst.

"Talia." My sister's hand comes down on my shoulder, instantly calming me. "Use the blood and let's get out of here and retrieve Tanya."

I take a deep breath and nod.

She's right.

It's what we came here to do, after all.

The possibility that it won't work is plaguing my mind.

But it's something I am willing to risk.

My life for Tanya's is something I will give any day.

"If it doesn't work, please tell her I tried."

"It *will* work. You can tell her yourself when you see her."

I want to believe her, but a part of me doesn't. Taking the vial from Patrick, they both step back as I walk to the barrier. My hands reach out and I feel the light buzz all over my skin when I touch it, like tiny pins and needles rushing everywhere throughout my body.

"As soon as it's down, she will know. And she *will* come looking for you," Bronik says.

I give him no reply. Instead, I open the vial and pour it into my hands as Viper told me to do when he whispered the spell. With my hands, now coated in someone else's blood, I reach out and start the spell.

"Tis will be broken, from blood to earth.
I take in with me each and every strand.
Tis will be broken, from sky to trees.
I take in with me each and every strand."

I chant it four times in total.

And at the end, my hands begin to shake and the blood starts to move from my hands as I whisper the last words once more.

"Blood to earth, it shall be done."

A large zap hits me, hard. I fall to the ground as every part of me feels as if it's on fire. Electrified. Charged.

I hear my name called, but my body refuses to move or to do anything. I try opening my eyes, but they don't want to move either. Then warm hands lift me from my back until my body isn't on the ground any longer.

"I've got her."

"Put her down. Now."

I know those voices, except my head isn't registering them properly, and my eyes don't want to open to see them either.

"She needs a minute."

Is that Bronik?

Taking a deep breath, my chest squeezes tight as hands lift me from the cold ground.

"Stop touching her," my sister growls.

"Should I drop her to the ground?" Bronik says back to my sister.

I hear her huff. "Talia, can you hear me?"

"Yes," I squeak. Managing to open my eyes, I look to find silver eyes locked on me. His eyes search mine for something. Whatever it is, he doesn't find it and looks away. My gaze remains on his face. His jawline is strongly defined. His tongue darts out, and he licks his lips slightly, which makes me tear my gaze from him before I start thinking of things other than why my body is aching.

"I think I can stand." Finally, I find enough strength to tell Bronik, and he gently places me down. I have to reach out and grip his shoulders so I don't fall, because my head is still spinning. Glancing down to my hand, which is now on my leg, the blood that was there is now completely gone.

"The spell took the blood," Bronik answers my unasked question.

"It's down. You did it." I look to see Patrick has already crossed the barrier and see him looking out over the hills. Not too far on the other side is the castle. I wonder if she will put more guards on this side now that the barrier is down. This is the most unprotected area, as no one has ever survived going through the Viper Forest, so her threat here has always been minimal. *But now that's changed.*

"Vampire," Patrick says in a fast voice before he jumps and turns into a wolf mid-air. His mouth opens, and as he closes it, a vampire appears between his teeth.

How the actual fuck?

The head rolls and lands before my feet as Patrick turns back, wiping the blood from his face and looking down the hill.

"Any more?" Tatiana asks, walking over to him.

I turn to Bronik. His silver eyes become darker, and it all happens in slow motion—his hand reaches out, he touches my arm, and boom! We are no longer standing on the edge of the forest. We are now in a white room with nothing else but him and me.

"Bronik." When my head stops spinning, I manage to rise to my feet and stare at him. This room is not unlike an empty, white box. "Where am I?"

He takes a step back and watches me. His eyes on

me are unnerving as he takes me in, not responding to me.

"Bronik."

"No one should have the power to control angels," he states.

I nod my head in agreement with him, feeling like I've made a grave mistake by listening to his direction. Something isn't right.

"And your power, well... it's natural, stronger. If she can control us... the most powerful beings on earth... what does that mean you can do?"

No. No way.

I would never do that.

But before I can speak, he goes on, "She wants me to bring you to her, but every part of me is saying otherwise. I don't know why I can see you so clearly when none of the other angels can. I don't know why they haven't broken from whatever spell she has put us under, but I believe I have. We are not meant to be down here. We had one job... create order, then leave. Yet we are still here years later."

This is all new information. I know nothing of this. I always assumed everything was as it seemed.

"The queen is not aware I can see past her spells, but I think you form part of that reason."

"Me?" My voice squeaks unusually high.

"Yes. It seems the more time I spend around you, the more it's breaking and the more I am seeing."

"I didn't do anything."

"No, I don't think you did." He walks in circles around me. "But that still doesn't make this decision easy. Either I kill you, or she does."

"Don't kill me," I beg of him, my legs now trembling.

"Do you think he would save you if I tried?" Bronik stands stock-still as he asks me the question I have no idea about, so I reply, "I don't know."

"I feel he wouldn't let me kill you. We both know he knows when it's your time to die, and I don't think it will be at my hands." He turns, and with a quick movement of his hand, the wall of one of the white rooms shows what looks like a television screen.

"She is very determined to keep you all alive." He eyes the screen where my sister is shown digging her hands into the earth and casting spells. The whole process is tiring her quickly. "One of you will die. It *will* happen." Then he snaps his fingers, and I am gone. I reappear standing near my sister. Once she sees me, she collapses with a soft smile on her face.

"John is going to kill me," Patrick mutters as he reaches for her.

I almost laugh.

Almost.

Chapter Eighteen

We wait because we have nothing else better to do. Patrick stands at the edge of the hill, making sure no more vampires come out to play as we wait for my sister to regain consciousness. Trying to find me after Bronik took me, took a lot out of her.

"Where did he take you?" Patrick asks, looking back at me.

"A room. I don't even know where it was located."

"*Wings.*"

My back straightens, and before I can say anything back, he appears in a cloud of dense, almost-black smoke in front of me.

"Oh, how I have missed you. I am glad to see you did not die." He notices my sister and raises a brow.

"She could have died and I would have been none the wiser." He smirks.

"I think it's best you shut up now," I bite back.

"Oh, Wings, why would I? I did help you, after all. Come on, Wings."

His black suit fits him well. Valefar is older, and from what I am aware, he likes to make deals. And with that knowledge, I know I should watch my words around him.

"We can always make a bargain. You know I can get your sister out of the castle. For a price, of course."

"What price?" I ask.

He looks at my sister and smiles. "A life for a life. She will do just fine. Powerful, that one, but not as powerful as you. Though, I do love to collect the souls of witches. They are always the feistiest."

My head starts shaking before the words have even left his mouth. "Not going to happen," I spit at him. "*Ever.*"

"You really are *no* fun." He turns and eyes Patrick, then looks back at me. "Enjoy your stay in Cardia. Do not let the queen *off your head.*" Then he is gone.

"You really attract all the weirdos," Patrick says.

I run my fingers through my sister's hair while she rests. "Well, I don't mean to. And if I remember correctly, it wasn't my idea to summon a demon."

"And now that you have, he doesn't seem to want to let go."

While the sun starts to rise as the moon falls from the sky, we sit and wait.

"John really will kill me if something happens to her," he says. "I only just survived the death of my mate. John will not, and that's saying something considering he is the strongest of us all. But the alpha's bond is also the most powerful. It feeds the pack and keeps them content."

"Tatiana has a way of always bouncing back," I say as she shifts around. "Let's get a bit of rest before we have to move again."

Patrick nods and sits on the other side of Tatiana, his head on his knees as he keeps a close watch.

"Do you love him?" Patrick asks me after silence fills the air.

"Who?" I question.

"Death. Do you love him?"

I turn away. "How can you love someone you don't even know?" I pause, giving my answer some thought. "He saves me, and for that I love him." It's all the answer I can give, and thankfully he doesn't push it any further. I lie back, keeping my sister on my lap as I close my eyes. My body is sore and tired from the running and the spell.

If I close my eyes for just a second…

* * *

"We have to go, Talia. Wake up, we have to move."

Dammit! I don't want to move! I want to stay asleep and not shift at all for the rest of the week. Haven't we done enough?

"Talia." Tatiana pushes me again, and I reluctantly open my eyes to find her hovering over me. "You need to get up. We slept."

"I know... we were tired." I stand and brush down my pants. "It's been a hell of a few days," I remind her. "Sometimes, we need to pass the hell out."

"Tanya is waiting for us."

"We have to get through the vampires first," Patrick says. "They and the angels have surrounded the castle. It's going to be a massive problem."

Tatiana turns to face me. "No holding back, at all."

I nod, my hands sweating from what could possibly come next.

"I mean it, Talia. The only way to get through this and to her is if you stop holding back."

It's hard listening to that when all my life I was told to be quiet, unassuming, and above all, never to use my powers because it may draw unwanted attention. And now I'm being told to do the complete opposite.

"I don't want to hurt anyone," I say, my voice small and wavering.

"It's too late for that now. Hurting is what needs to be done. Wars weren't won with people being cordial, Talia. Be cruel, vindictive, ruthless. You need to be worse than the queen to defeat the queen."

"You want me to kill the queen?"

"No, that job will be mine." She turns and looks out, pocketing her knife as she smiles, and the joy touches her eyes.

"You should be queen," I state, and I believe it, as I always have. Tatiana is a born leader. People would listen to her, where I am certain no one will listen to me.

Tatiana shakes her head. "I would never want to. Besides, it's not me who is meant to be queen. And every queen needs a fierce warrior by her side. It just so happens I'm yours." She winks and starts walking. Patrick follows her, and I begrudgingly do the same.

We stay close to the trees and keep watch, but it's hard when vampires are known for their strength, speed, and agility.

"Wings." We all stop as Valefar appears in front of us. "Vampire coming in... 3, 2, 1..." Just as he finishes his countdown, a vampire appears behind him. His red eyes are set on me as it walks at a slow pace, its eyes hungry for something. I glance at my sister, but she's not moving and Patrick's frozen at her side. "They will be of no help. All they can do is watch," the demon says, condescension lacing his tone.

I take a step back, and my hands come to my sides to protect myself, palms open, ready to fight.

"Tsk tsk. You need more than that, silly girl." The vampire pays Valefar's words no mind, as he slowly makes his way toward us. Then another appears, coming up the hill and directly at me.

Two of them.

Fuck.

My odds of winning this battle are low.

Searching, I find Tatiana is still unable to move. When I look back at Valefar, he seems to be enjoying watching me struggle and wondering what I'm going to do next. The asshole is taking great pleasure in watching this play out in front of him.

"Use your power, Wings. Don't be silly."

"I'll kill them," I whisper as the vampire reaches me.

The vampire is not fazed by my words.

I hear the demon laughing, but I can't say anything back because the vampire is practically on me and those sharp teeth come dangerously close to my neck. I just manage to pull him back off me, but he is fast, and within a blink, I feel his teeth touch my skin and everything in me goes cold like ice. The world seems to slow, and my hands, that were at my sides, reach up and touch the vampire. His teeth don't move to bite and the rest of him is still.

I feel the power flow through me as the other vampire reaches me. I feel his indecision on whether or not to attack me, but he thinks with blood rather than logic. He comes up, and the minute he touches me, I freeze him too. Every part of me comes alive, and it's nothing like I have experienced before. I have played with my powers, but never to this extent. I only learned the basics, like every other witch. But this stuff? This stuff is all brand-new and coming to me so easily.

I take a deep breath, my hands, which are now on each of the vampires' shoulders, press harder into them before I feel the power leave them. Their life force they hold so dear, the force that keeps them alive, flows from their bodies and makes its way into mine. It's like snakes slithering up my arms until the strength reaches my chest. My eyes fly open, and my head drops back. I feel my eyes change, and somehow I know it's the color. How I know? I have no clue, but I am positive they are no longer my usual emerald-green color that matches my sisters'.

I have no idea what they look like now.

I feel the vampires' bodies drop to the ground before they turn to ash. I'm not sure how I did it, or what I even did to cause their destruction. It's not like how I borrow power, it was more like me stealing it to end them.

Hands clap to the left of me. When my eyes land on the person clapping, I have the urge to reach out and do the same thing to him that I just did to the vamps.

"Look how powerful you are. It's a beautiful thing to witness." He smirks, then disappears.

"Talia." I turn to see my sister behind me, her eyes firmly set on the pile of ashes at my feet. When her gaze makes its way to my face, her eyes widen in surprise and she blinks a few times. "Your eyes, they are ice blue."

I blink, again, then again until I feel them change back.

"How... h-how is that possible?"

"I didn't mean to..." I reply. It was something that had to be done—them or me. And I do not want to die tonight and especially not with my blood being drained by them, that's for sure.

"We don't have time to waste," Patrick says. "Can we discuss this later? Maybe when I don't hear plenty of running footsteps coming straight for us?" Patrick shakes and shifts into his wolf form. I look back to my sister to see her watching me carefully.

"You would wake up sometimes with those eyes.

You would also make me float from my bed while I was asleep."

She's never told me this before.

"It's the wolves," I say, taking a deep breath. Patrick looks back at me before he sniffs the air and runs ahead. "Tatiana, am I a..." I don't know how to say it, "...a monster?"

She shakes her head while her warm hands touch my arm. "Never, ever. It's impossible for you to be that way. If any of us were, it would be me, for sure." She offers me a smile but the sadness in her eyes gives it away.

As John reaches her, he grabs hold, making sure she is still intact. She doesn't protest, and I can tell she's exhausted. Not so much physically, but emotionally spent. I don't blame her. We never asked for this life, yet we are forced to live it.

"You can put me down now." I watch their interaction. John looks back to me and smiles before he locks eyes again with Tatiana. He has her off the ground, his hands around her, and as he slowly places her back down, he always makes sure to keep touching her, even when she turns to look around.

"Plans have changed," John says.

I eye him, not understanding what he's talking about. All the wolves from his pack are now standing here with us, some quiet, and others not so much. Half of them didn't like us to begin with, and now they seem even angrier.

"What are you talking about? The Crystal Castle is less than a day's walk, possibly half if we move fast." Tatiana turns in the direction we are meant to go but is held in place by John.

"She knows you are coming," John says. "And because of this, she has moved your sister."

We both stare at him.

"Is she hurt?" I ask.

"As far as we are aware, your sister has been put under a spell. She tried to escape, and the queen locked her in a barrier cage."

"What?" I say, surprised. "Tanya would never hurt her, why would she do that?" Barrier cages hurt if you move. Touch the edges and your whole body feels like it's been electrified, it's worse than the barriers between the wards. The queen knows Tanya, knows she would never hurt anyone or do anything to cause harm. Yet she treats her as if she is a villain who is set to destroy her world. I guess that tells me everything I need to know about the queen, including her motivations.

"Talia." My sister says my name, but I ignore her as anger takes hold of me. How could the queen be so cruel? So mean? The little I remember of her growing up, she was never this cold, and never calculated. Yes, I know all the stories of who she is now. But being a victim of it is different from hearing about it. And her villainy is now happening to my sister of all people.

"Little fighter." When I look around, I see Grim standing in front of me, but he hasn't frozen time like he usually does. My eyes scan him before I look past him to my sister.

"Talia."

I ignore my sister's voice and look back at Grim. "Why are you here? You could be saving her, and here you are. So... save her." His usually calm face drops for just a second before it goes straight back in place, but I saw it. *Pain.* "They can see you, hear you," I say to him and look around. Everyone is staring at him like their eyes cannot believe what they are seeing.

"You have control this time, I do not."

I shake my head at his words and my eyebrows automatically pull in. "That doesn't make sense," I utter.

A warm sensation in my palms draws my attention, and when I glance down, my hands are ablaze. Fire coats them and Grim steps forward, putting them out with his touch. His hand then lifts and touches my face. "I need you to calm down." I shake my head, the emotions are still too much, they're overwhelming me. "Little fighter..." I want to argue with him, but his hand is stroking my face, and as I close my eyes at his touch, I feel the world shift. When I open them again, we are standing near the sea, the waves hitting the beach, and it's just the two of us.

"I don't want to be here."

"But here you are, little fighter..." He smirks, and I turn away.

Chapter Nineteen

When I manage to turn back around and face him, he's watching me with those silver eyes.

"I had to remove you from the situation," he says before I can open my mouth. "You would never forgive yourself for hurting those you love." He's right. I never, ever would. I would rather die a hundred deaths than hurt those I love.

"Could I kill you?" I ask.

He walks up behind me, and I feel his breath on my neck as he leans down. I want him to kiss me, and I shiver at that thought.

A kiss from Death himself.

What a way to die.

"I believe you could do anything you set your

mind to. You are *that* powerful. It's one of the reasons I am drawn to you."

I spin and look at him. "What are the others?"

He obliges and smirks, showing his perfect white teeth and a dimple cast in his flawless face. How can he have the most defined jaw structure? It's so sharp that if you ran your tongue along it, you may very well cut yourself.

And I want to cut myself.

On him.

"It started off as a curiosity. Who is this being that keeps on getting herself in tricky situations?" His lip twitches at the thought of me almost hurting or killing myself and him always saving me. "Then it grew to something else, which you do *not* need to know."

"Why?" I want to know. I inch closer, our bodies touching. The urge to wrap my hands around him and pull him to me so no air can escape is strong.

I feel these things for him.

I want to do these things to him.

So many dirty things.

He looks into my eyes, and if I hadn't looked into his a hundred times before, I would look away at the power they hold. But I have, and I can tell that despite how hard they look, he is kind. To me, at least. To others, perhaps not.

Cold hands brush my face before they fall ever so

slowly down my cheeks, dragging along my neck before they land on my hips. He grips me, and I feel myself only thinking of him.

How can his touch drive me so mad? It's a simple touch, yet it makes my insides scream with madness.

Madness for him.

"Some things are better left unsaid."

I reach out and graze his hip, and he doesn't pull away.

I can feel him between my legs, our bodies that close. Would it be wrong if I started to move to see what he would do? If I touched him between his legs... Would he need me, or want me, the same way I want him?

"Tell me," I demand. I lean up on my tippy-toes, ready to kiss him, to feel his lips for the first time, but he stops me, his finger reaching out and touching my lips.

"It's time for you to go now, little fighter."

I open my mouth to argue with him, but before I can, I am back where we left from and everyone is looking at me like I've grown a second head, which I know I haven't.

John has Tatiana around the waist as if he is holding her back, and when she spots me, she instantly calms and he lets her go.

"You aren't allowed to do that again." Tatiana

reaches for me, but when she touches me, she swears and pulls her hand away.

"What?" I ask her, confused.

"You are like fire. Look…" She shows me her hand and I can see the red marking from where she touched me. Everyone is quiet as they watch me.

"What am I?" I ask her softly, so my voice doesn't crack or break. "Grim touched me, and I didn't hurt him," I tell her. "So why did I hurt you?"

Tatiana looks back to John, who walks over and touches my shoulder, and when he does, he pulls away just as quickly as Tatiana did.

"Fuck, you are literally like fire."

"What does that even mean?" I ask, my voice becoming shrill with fear.

My sister appears worried for a second before she turns away. "We have to get Tanya. We can work it all out after that. I'm sure it's nothing bad, Talia. Your power has been through a lot more than you're used to. Let's come up with a plan, then we go from there."

I nod because right now that's all I can do.

She watches me while the group listens as John starts speaking. I want to lean on her shoulder, to tell her I love her, but I can't. I'm too afraid I may hurt her, or worse, kill her. I am craving her comforting touch, yearning for the attention that I desperately seek right now. There is simply no way to risk it. At this moment, I am on my own, and the only person I can touch without hurt and destruction is Death himself. How peculiar—it goes against everything logical and within reason.

Slowly, I step closer to her and lean in enough so only she can hear me, but not close enough to actually touch her.

"Are you afraid of me?"

Her eyes go wide at my words. "No, never."

I know she means it, but it doesn't make me feel any better. Touch is something I crave, but I know right now, it's off the table.

"I didn't mean to. Before..." I don't even know what it was, or how to even discuss it. All I do know is I couldn't control it a second longer.

"I know. And that's something we will work on at a later date. You know I will do anything in my power to help you. But right now, Tanya needs us."

I know she's right, it needs to be less about being in my own head right now and more about being here. When I focus back on our surroundings, I see that everyone was listening to our conversation.

Shit! Wolf hearing, I forgot about that.

John starts talking again, and all eyes go back to him.

"We have no home anymore, and you still expect us

to help them?" one of the wolves says, the edge in their voice full of resentment.

I try to keep my head low as they sort it out. But I lean over to Patrick who is now sitting next to me in the grass, his knees up, watching his alpha intently.

"What happened to your home?"

"You happened." An angry wolf glares at me. It's the same woman from the night we arrived on their land. Clearly, she wants no business with us. "If you hadn't entered our land, demanded that we help you, and taken our alpha away, we wouldn't be here." She's angry, and the angrier she gets, the closer she steps toward me.

"I didn't take your alpha," I say.

She growls, showing me her teeth.

"You and that thing you call a sister did. Do not lie to us, witch."

I stand, Patrick mirroring my movement next to me.

"You even took our beta. Do you have no respect at all?"

"If you believe I have the power to take something from you, was it even yours to begin with?" I ask, because as far as I'm concerned, I took no one. And I'm not going to let everyone think they can walk over me.

She growls and jumps toward me. I move forward

and let her hand touch my skin. I can feel the burn from where her nails dig in, but I don't back away. I stay there until she screams seconds later.

"You belong in the depths of hell. You will be no better than that evil thing we call a queen." She backs up, cradling her hand, as my sister steps closer and inspects my arm.

"I'm okay," I tell her, but she isn't listening.

She turns and faces the angry wolf. "Think about doing that again and I will end your life, right here where you stand. Do. You. Understand. Me?"

I go to reach for my sister but think better of it and pull my hand back. The last thing I want to do is hurt her.

"You... you are the first I will kill." The wolf jumps for my sister, and in mid-air, she is caught by the throat in her wolf form by John. I watch in shock as John squeezes the wolf's throat, making her yelp, before lowering her to the ground but keeping his hands around her neck. As the alpha, even in his human form, he is stronger than most.

"If any of you..." John looks around to every wolf who is present, then continues with everyone's attention, "...think you can get away with harming my mate, you are truly misguided. I will end your life the minute you think about it. This will be my first and only warning." He turns back to the wolf he still holds in his grasp, his muscles bulging as he squeezes a little tighter. "You can leave, and take whoever holds your beliefs with you. You ever think of returning or harming either of these women, I will end you faster than you can say sorry." He drops her and she falls to the ground, shifting back to her human form.

John steps back until he is standing next to Tatiana again, and she leans into him and looks at me behind his back, smiling.

Oh, she likes him, all right. A lot.

"You're choosing a *witch* over your pack?" another wolf barks out.

"I'm choosing *my mate*. And you would be wise to stop whatever you are about to say about her. My temper is currently running exceedingly high."

The woman stands, and her hands go to her neck as she looks at John, then she turns, walking away from the pack the same way she came.

"Anyone going with her? Because if you choose to stay, you *will* respect my mate and her sister." A few people whisper, but no one else moves. "Good. Now, let's work out a plan of attack."

We all go silent as John sits back down as if nothing happened. He grabs a stick and starts drawing the castle in the dirt at his feet. "Here." He points to the back of the castle. "This spot is only guarded by one vampire. The angels don't guard outside the castle...

they are all inside. They will be an issue, as we aren't sure yet how to defeat them," John says.

Then he points to the front of the castle. "Six vampires were guarding yesterday, more than the usual two we were told she usually has on her. She is expecting you." John looks at me. "I think it's time you explore your powers a little more. We need every chance we can get to be able to enter. Because that's where it will be tricky." He takes a deep breath. "It could very much be a suicide mission."

"So why even do it? Surely one girl's life is no more important than hundreds of ours?" one of the wolves yells.

The problem is—they are right.

But I didn't ask them to come.

Tatiana and I would do it ourselves if we had to. Tanya will be relying on us to protect her, and as a family, we will do exactly that.

"It's not just about one girl. Yes, she is a bonus, but it's more than that. Queen Veronica has ruled long enough, and it's time for her reign to come to an end." A few people cheer in response to John's words while others stay silent.

He turns to face me. "We know you can turn a vampire to ash. What else can you do?" I look to my sister, who bites her lip. "Tatiana?" he asks her. "You can trust me. You know you can."

"I can trust you, yes. But the lives of my sisters are not something I ever want to put in jeopardy or into anyone else's hands. My parents left me in charge, and protecting them is what I want to do until my dying breath."

"I can do almost anything you think of, being supernatural," I say, so she doesn't have to defend me.

John stares at me as if he doesn't believe me.

Then, one of the wolves whispers, "Demon."

I always knew I would be cast as one. Just from my limited powers that I have tested, they match those of a demon. But all demons serve in hell and are tied to it, whereas I serve no one and live my own life.

"No, she is a witch. A witch with incredibly special gifts, that's for sure. So, you have all four elements, plus other powers?" John asks.

I nod, not denying it.

Tatiana is gifted with earth, and she is extraordinarily strong using her gift. Tanya is gifted with air, but she doesn't like to practice so her powers are limited.

"Is that why you are hot to touch right now?"

"Fire witch," Patrick says. "Like those in the forest... half fire witch, half fairy." I nod. There aren't any fire witches left other than the three in the Viper Forest, and I was never going to announce myself. We caused too much chaos in the past when we got angry. Whole cities would catch on fire if we became enraged.

It's what happened before, but I wasn't going to admit that.

Being an earth witch, like our mother was, would have been easier.

Having all four elements isn't heard of, let alone spoken about. And on top of that, I have other abilities I cannot even comprehend. Yet, they are there.

"I'm not sure I can turn more than three vampire into ash at a time... it drains me doing one let alone two." I turn the discussion back over to John, and he nods and looks around.

"We can handle the vampires. It's the angels I'm more worried about. No one has ever taken one down. They are stronger, smarter, and can do things we cannot."

We know this, but it won't stop my sister and me from trying to enter to save Tanya. I just hope all the wolves are not killed in the process.

Chapter Twenty

John talks, people listen. I guess that's what it means to be an alpha. He makes a plan and that's when we attack.

We wait. When John gives the go-ahead, Tatiana doesn't argue with him, even though I know she wants to. She is so used to being in charge that it's weird for her to have someone else take the lead.

It's not even that I need her to be in charge, but I like her to be. I'm old enough to fend for myself, live by myself, but our world has changed so much that it's smarter to stick together.

I watch them, how John stays by her side, not moving an inch away from her. When she takes a heavy breath, I feel him stop while he watches her.

Their love is going to move mountains, change lives, and be something wonderful to witness.

While mine...

"Little fighter." I freeze at his voice. When I look up, I see him standing in front of me, his hands to his sides. "Your thoughts are powerful," he says, and I make no attempt to move as he stands above me, untouchable.

"Why did you come?" I ask.

Everyone around us is frozen because we are in his time right now. His lip lifts just a fraction before he pulls it between his teeth and it pops back out. Does he even realize what he is doing?

"If I kissed you now, would you stop me?" I ask him, suddenly overwhelmed by a new feeling of confidence, unafraid to finally ask for what I've been craving for so long.

"Probably not." His answer surprises me.

"So why do you not kiss me?"

He turns and looks up to the heavens and holds his head there for a few seconds before his silver eyes find mine and he speaks, "Because I am *not* your future. I would be temporary."

"How can you even know that?" I ask tentatively. "You know death, you do not know my future."

"But I see who is with you when you die, little fighter." His words are like ice running all over my body. "And it is not me."

The final sting.

That hurt.

"So, there is one time you cannot save me." I force a smile as I look at him.

He nods once.

I crawl toward him, on my hands and knees. He gets down to my level, and as he does, I crawl onto his lap. I can feel him beneath me, touching every part of me. He is hard, and I wonder if he knows what to do with it? Do angels have sex?

"You can't always save me," I say, leaning in. His hands wrap around my waist, and I lean forward, ready to kiss him, but at the last minute, I turn my head and my lips meet his neck. His skin is cold beneath my lips, and as I push myself forward onto him, I can feel his hardness between us. I bite my lip to stop the soft moan that wants to leave.

"What is it that you are doing, little fighter?" His voice has changed, being more huskier now. Dirtier. Did I do that to him?

"I do not know," I answer him truthfully.

I stop and pull away, putting distance between us. He moves forward and pushes my hair back behind my ear.

"I'm going to give you something, something that is forbidden. You must not tell anyone and use it at your discretion." He pulls out a sharp blade. It's small, bright, and looks a lot like other knives, but there is something incredibly different about it. I stand, wiping the dirt off my ass before I face him again. In those eyes that hold death, I see anything but. I see someone who is like no other person I have ever met. Someone I probably should have never met, but someone I was destined for.

I see death in all he's beauty.

Stepping forward until I am almost touching him again, I reach for the knife. My hand grazes his and our eyes lock.

"Why are you giving me this?" I take hold and it sends a buzz all through my body. I feel a weird connection with it, and when he removes his hand, I blink a few times at the loss.

He seems puzzled at first, his brows knit together as he stares at it.

"What does this do?"

"It kills angels," he answers.

My fingers open and it drops to the ground at my feet. I take a step back and stare down at it, at the power it holds.

"The problem... only you can use it but no one else can. Do you understand me?"

"No." I start shaking my head. "I definitely do not understand you at all. How is this even a thing?" I glance back to the blade shining brightly in the dirt, and I lean down to pick it up and hold it in my hands again, feeling the uniqueness.

"It is not known by humankind or supernaturals. This is only used by us. We keep our weapons under wraps. But those angels you are facing are no longer serving the same god I am, so this is why I give you this weapon. They will not care if they end your life. And I would rather avoid that if I can."

"How chivalrous of you," I say with an eyeroll.

"Don't mistake me for a caring man, little fighter. I am neither man nor caring."

"You care if I die."

His lips thin at my words. "I do."

Before I can stop myself or talk myself out of it, I lean forward and my lips connect with his. He doesn't stop me, doesn't pull away. He lets me have this moment for whatever it will be worth. One of my hands grips the back of his neck while he just stands there. He doesn't kiss me back, and because of that, I go to pull away. As I do, his hands snake around my waist and pull me to him so our bodies are smashed together, the knife somewhere between us, as he holds me as if I am his everything.

Then he moves his lips. Those sinful, full lips melt into mine and open as he takes everything I can give. He kisses me back with the most soulful kisses, as if he collected them and waited until this perfect moment to give them to me.

I take it because, for once, I want to be greedy.

Greedy with Death.

Even saying the words makes me question my sanity.

My hands at his neck claw at him, needing more and never wanting this to end. When our tongues touch, it feels like a hundred fireworks just went off in my stomach. This is what it should always feel like, and I'll never be able to forget it now.

I've been kissed before.

Slow.

Rough.

Kind.

But never with a fierceness that takes hold of my body and grips to my soul with its dark clutches and won't let go.

To stop him would be a sin.

To have him would be death, floating up to heaven.

I can't imagine what that would be like, so I relish all that he is willing to grant me right now. His mouth on mine, his tongue dancing with mine, giving me something he has denied or not parted with before.

He tastes like cotton candy and fresh air, like salt-water mixed with the perfect alcohol. You can't help but lick your lips at his taste. And tasting him is what I am doing, what I plan to do every time I see him.

Then, as quickly as it started, he is gone.

And I am left standing there, the knife still in one hand, the world going back to normal, the air flicking at my hair, and trying to remember to catch my breath and steady my rapidly beating heart.

A heart that beats for Death. Only Death.

What have I gotten myself into?

"Talia."

I turn to my sister. She tries to see what's in my hand, but I slide it into my jacket and lean over to whisper in her ear. "Death," is all I say, then I pull back and hold a finger up to my mouth, whispering, "Shhh."

She nods, knowing full well not to speak of it.

"Why are you flushed?" she asks me, changing the subject.

Dropping my head back, I look up to the night sky. Tomorrow at first light, we move toward the queen's castle.

"He kissed me. Well, I kissed him."

"That was your first time kissing him?" she asks, sounding somewhat surprised. I give her a confused look. "You really have never kissed him before?"

"No, I told you... he only appears when I need him." I shrug, and John comes and sits next to her.

"How was it? The kiss?" she asks, smiling now. "Was it hot? I bet it was hot. He is pretty fucking fine." She smiles, which makes me smile, and John simply grunts next to her, obviously not wanting to overhear this conversation.

"It was..." I don't even know how to put it into words. "He said he wasn't my destiny and that's why he's never done anything before."

"Destinies are meant to be broken, baby." She winks, and John pulls her to him and sits her between his legs.

I lie down and close my eyes.

And dream of Death.

* * *

The wolves wake at the crack of dawn, leaving no time for hesitation. I hide the knife that Grim gave me in my jacket, keeping it close. It can't fall into the wrong hands. Of that I am sure. Plus, he gave it to me to use to help my sister. That is all.

"You ready?" Patrick asks. He's now wearing jeans and a button-up shirt. I nod before he speaks again. "I'm going to shadow you. Where you go, I go."

"Is that John's order?"

"And your sister's," he adds, looking back over to where they are standing. They are lost in conversation but both look our way before John nods to Patrick and turns to talk to the wolves. "Talia." He touches my arm, and I realize I'm not hot to touch anymore which makes me smile. "Are you okay?"

I don't even know how to answer that question.

What does it even mean to be okay?

Am I okay? No.

Will I ever be again? I don't know.

I just want my sister back.

I want to live in a world where I trust it won't come at me and possibly kill me. Because this world right now, we cannot trust.

"Tatiana," I call out.

Patrick stays behind me as I catch up with my sister. She turns, stepping from her spot next to John, where he instructs his wolves, and waits for me. "I have something..." She raises a brow at my words. I lean in close and whisper in her ear, "I have something that will kill an angel." I don't trust anyone else with that information, hence why it is only for her ears and why I am speaking so softly. I don't want anyone to overhear.

"How..." She shakes her head. "Did Death... he gave it to you?" I nod my head. "Okay, well... keep that to yourself. That's not something that should be shared."

"Should we..." I nod to John.

She looks over her shoulder to where he stands, pauses to think, then looks back to me. "No. It's yours. It was given to you. So, no." A slice of worry etches over her brows, but it's gone before I can think too much about it.

The barriers are all down, but that was only one of our concerns. Now we have *a lot* more. All the supernaturals they were holding back are now free to roam where they will. Vampires are free to attack, witches are no longer confined to their own ward. But the angels, well, they will continue to serve the queen as has always been.

"Let's go. If you see or hear anything unusual, let me know straight away. *Do not,* I repeat, *do not* attack anything without someone with you. We may be able to kill a vampire, but remember who they have on their side." Everyone listens to John, and I watch as they take in his words. He doesn't hold his leadership and power over their heads like our queen does. He respects his people and speaks to them all as if they are his friends.

Tatiana walks over to him, and I wonder if she even knows what she's doing. She cannot deny the fact that she is drawn to him. Before this, you would never have gotten her to leave my side, and now she is walking over and touching the small of his back. His hand reaches behind him and clutches hers as he continues to talk to a few wolves.

I watch as she visibly relaxes at his touch.

Will I ever have that? I want what they have—to love somebody and be loved in return unconditionally.

Witches marry witches, it's how the world works.

Wolves marry wolves, it's how it's been done for centuries.

Yet, here my sister is, falling for an alpha wolf who picked her as his mate.

The world is clearly changing, and I can't help but wonder if I have something to do with that.

Chapter Twenty-One

The sun falls behind the earth and the night sky is nothing but blackness, as if it's ready and waiting for us to strike. Does it know what is coming? What is about to happen? How many lives that could be lost in this process?

That's not something I want to think about, but it's not something that leaves my mind either.

Death.

And not my Death. No, he will outlive all of us.

"They have the advantage during the night," I hear one of the wolves complain as we all start walking. The closer we get to the castle, the colder I seem to get.

I'm half-listening and half looking ahead to check where we're going. But as one of the female wolves turns back and looks to another, I see something. It's small, almost like a glimmer, so I stop and narrow my eyes, but the wolves don't even pause. As she gets closer, I watch in absolute horror as her body hits the glimmer and is cleaved in half, literally.

"Stop." My voice is loud, and everyone does just that, apart from the wolves at the front who have just seen their friend sliced in half. Not the half separating the top half of her body from the bottom, but vertically straight down the middle. They scream and start to run back to us. I look closely as the glimmer shimmers even brighter then turns black.

It's a wall of blackness.

Not like the barriers. No, this one is more lethal.

"She can't have that type of magic. That's most definitely *not* witch magic," my sister says. Stepping closer, she lifts her hand up, but I reach her and pull her back.

"Don't touch it," I say to her softly.

I hear some of the wolves crying behind me as Patrick comes to stand next to me. "I've seen this once," he says. He looks back to John, who nods in agreement. "When they created the borders, the wolves didn't take kindly to them, so this here was put up for a short amount of time to keep us where they wanted us. It was there until the barriers were created." He turns to me. "This is demon magic."

"Of course it is," my sister curses. "Does she have a

demon in her back pocket or something and just rubs him to make her damn wishes come true?"

"Well, I don't really like to be rubbed. But if you are offering." We turn to see a demon standing behind us. And not just any demon, but the one that keeps popping up. "How's your day been, Wings? Any developments on saving your sister?" he asks as John curses at him for even speaking about my sister.

Tatiana touches John's shoulder to soothe him as the demon clicks his fingers and the dead body disappears. "Ugly thing to look at, right? I don't like to look at death." A shiver runs over his body and he smiles. "I'm willing to help break this wall," Valefar says, eyeing me.

"What is the price?" Tatiana aks, and he clicks his tongue at her.

"Too clever. You are too clever." The demon steps to the wall, places his palm on it, and doesn't get singed or cut in half.

"I want you for one night," Valefar says, then locks his eyes on me.

My mind can't register what he is saying.

Did he?

What the fuck!

"Do you think I am a whore?" I ask him in disbelief.

I hear the soft chants from behind me and see my

sister giving the demon a death stare, her eyes cast on him as she says a spell.

"Knock it off, witch, your magic will not harm me," he says, as if it's a joke, and laughs before he looks back to me. "It's not for sex. I simply wish to spend an evening with you."

"Nothing sexual?" I ask, clarifying.

"Nothing. Unless you ask for it, that is." He winks, and I nod my head, looking past him to the wall, which is impenetrable. "Break it."

"No can do. A door is all I can manage." He waves his hand and, just as he said, a door appears. "Tick-tock. You have exactly one minute before it starts to close. And be prepared, she's waiting and setting traps as we speak. She wants you dead and will do anything in her power to see that through."

I walk forward and decide I should be the first to step through. Valefar watches me with eager eyes, as if he thinks I may not do it. But, of course, I will, I don't want to see anyone else die because of me. Taking a deep breath, I take the first step, and when nothing happens, I keep on moving through.

"Talia." I turn as my name is called to see my sister on the other side.

"Fast, witch," Valefar says, then disappears.

Tatiana enters after me and the wolves follow. I see

the door start to close as the last wolf jumps through, closing completely once she is fully through the opening.

"Can you believe…"

The loudest sound I have ever heard hisses behind us. The ground begins to shake, and Patrick, who is next to me, puts his hand on my shoulder. "We must move, fast."

I nod and nobody needs to be told twice. We all begin moving and enter into territory we don't really want to venture into, but have absolutely no choice.

"Oh, she will be happy with me. Maybe I can have my own castle, too." A single vampire materializes from the darkness. He licks his sharp teeth. "Clean up the trash." He nods, and behind him appears two more vampires, not young ones either. They are more powerful, clever, and shrewd. But we have a whole pack of wolves, and I have seen one wolf tear a vampire to shreds, so I'm not that concerned. Until…

"Talia." Tatiana is next to me in a flash, her back to me as she comes closer, her hands out, ready to drop to the ground to use her magic.

"You really didn't think there would be only a few of us, did you?" the vampire teases. And that's when I see what has my sister so worried. Standing behind her, where we just came from, are over twenty vampires, all ready to tear our heads from our bodies and hand us over to the queen, dead or alive, it matters not.

They hiss, their steps silent as they take each one toward us menacingly.

I've seen vampires, several times, but this many focused on us with hungry eyes is something I've never had to deal with before.

"I see you made it out of the forest alive..." he starts, then laughs, "...only to be killed by us. I bet right now you wish you died in there." The one vampire that's doing all the talking is looking between my sister and me. Her hand clutches mine, and I know what she's asking me to do—to borrow her power.

Patrick walks over and his hand grasps my shoulder. He is telling me to do the same thing.

But...

"I've always wanted to play with a witch... fuck one... make her bleed so we can taste her, and then fuck her some more before she bleeds all over my tongue." I try not to gasp at his words. No vampire I have met has ever once spoken like this. Actually, no one has. I know what kink is, but I have never experienced such things and I am unsure I ever want to.

"You'd be surprised to know I would slit your throat and make you bleed before you even had the chance to do that to me," Tatiana says from behind me, her hand still grasped in mine.

He smirks, holds his hand to his chest, and throws his head back in laughter. We stare, shocked, until he suddenly stops, and his eyes turn a fiery red as he pins them on Tatiana.

"You will be the last kept alive. I'll bleed you so many times that by the end, you will be begging for me to slit your throat if you don't have the courage to do it yourself."

A loud snarl tears from the middle of our group, and we watch as John transforms and turns his attention to the vampire.

"Here, kitty kitty," the vampire teases.

The other wolves stay where they are, surrounding us, as John does just that. He jumps and goes straight for the vampire's throat. But as he is a mere inch from him, he is captured. A man in a white cloak grabs John by the muzzle, grips it hard, then so fast that if we blinked we would miss it, he throws him as if he were just that, a little tiny kitty.

Bronik wipes his hands on his white suit before he looks back up, his eyes searching before they land on me.

"It's always a pleasure, Talia. Now, if you would accompany me to the queen, your friends may not have to die today."

The wolves start howling and transforming—all but Patrick, whose hand is still on my shoulder.

Tatiana's hand is now squeezing mine so tightly, I think the blood has stopped circulating in my fingers.

"You," I say in shock. "Why?" I ask, staring at Bronik in complete disbelief. I thought I could trust him, but I guess I was very wrong.

"I needed to test your abilities for the queen. Seems you are stronger than we anticipated." He looks to Tatiana and smiles. "As are you, but I haven't shared that secret with your old friend yet." As he finishes speaking, another angel appears right next to Bronik.

"Time's a-wasting." He steps forward before Bronik does and comes toward me. I freeze for a moment, but that's all an angel needs. In the blink of an eye, he has thrown all the wolves in his path out the way, the same way Bronik did to John.

Fuck! John. Is he dead?

No, he can't be.

Tatiana stays where she is, gripped to me, as is Patrick.

"He may like to play games with you, but I will do no such thing, little witch." The other angel reaches out to touch me, and as he does, I grab hold of the knife—the knife that Death gave me—and slide it up out of hiding while the angel's eyes are on mine, slipping it between us as he grabs my arm, painfully. In one swift movement, I jab it straight into his chest, and instantly his hand leaves my arm. His face turns into a soft smile before he looks up to the sky, and in the next moment... he is ash. I wasn't sure where to stab, but it seems the chest works. Grim should have given me clearer instructions.

"How..." A vampire hisses, breaking my concentration on the pile of ash, trying to work out how it happened.

But there isn't time to waste.

We are badly outnumbered.

I pull all the air I can take into my lungs before I reach for my power. It's like birds singing in the sky—a worm finding its hole.

It feels like home.

No other place feels like this or feels this good.

Except...

I can't think of him. Death. We could never work. And soon, I could very well be dead anyway.

"Do you see?" I hear the vampire say.

The sound of footsteps echoes around us, louder than before. It's as if every step is amplified and only I can hear it. I hear the heartbeats of the wolves, and when I take a deep breath, I know John is still alive. Injured but alive.

Opening my eyes, Bronik is standing there watching me with a smile on his face, as if he's excited to see what I am about to do. I don't even know what it is, but I feel it. I feel the pull to reach out to every dead vampire here right now and snatch their power because they should not exist. They should be banished just as we have been for years.

I want to do worse, though.

So much worse.

Smiling, I let it go. It's like snakes wriggling all over my body, lightly massaging as they go free, searching for their target. I feel when they grip onto who they are searching for, then they pull, the same way a vampire does pulling life from a vein.

"Extraordinary," Bronik remarks in a whisper.

Two people drop to the ground, my sister and Patrick both unconscious as they fall. The only ones left standing are me, Bronik, and the vampire who promised to fuck my sister up.

I kept him alive for her because all the others are dead.

And by the look of horror that crosses his face, I know he knows it as well.

"Get me out of here." The vampire turns to Bronik who simply smirks at me.

"You lied," I say to him, feeling all that power creep back up my body and slithering its way back to where it belongs. He goes back and forth, so whose team is he really on?

"I did, and it was worth it." He winks, then he's gone.

I blow a spell at the vampire to keep him in place, sticking his feet to the ground, as I turn and head back to my sister.

"Tatiana." I lay a hand on her, trying to be as gentle as possible. She knew what she was doing. We have trained before, but I have never taken that much power. Reaching for her hand, I push her power back to try and recharge her. She is so vital to who I am, what I am, that if I ever did anything to actually hurt her, I'm not sure how I would cope. Or how I would even survive such a disaster.

When I finally see the flutter of her lashes, I reach for Patrick's hand and do the same. He wakes faster than Tatiana did and sits up straight away, transforming into a wolf and stilling.

"Are you okay?" I ask Tatiana, but she doesn't answer. Instead, she blinks a few times and starts looking around.

"Tatiana."

Her head swings around and she finds John. I step back as she crawls—no energy left in her—until she reaches him. Her hand touches his first, and the moment it does, he pulls her into him and cradles her as if she is his everything.

She is.

He is.

They are each other's everything.

And that right there only goes to prove that in a world so dark, so fucked up, light can be seen through the smallest of cracks, and if you really look hard enough, you may be able to find it.

Chapter Twenty-Two

Some are injured but none are dead, apart from the angel and vampires. The one vampire who taunted us remains where he is, unable to move. My sister is now standing and so is John. I can see the limp in his leg where it was either broken or badly hurt. He's not shapeshifting back into his wolf form, though, as Patrick did to heal faster. His hand hasn't left my sister since he got her back by his side.

"You shouldn't exist, you are an abomination," the vampire hisses at me.

"I guess your queen told you that?" I ask.

He laughs and throws his head back. "No, bitch, I don't need her to tell me, I can see it with my own eyes. No one should have that much power."

"But your queen can?" I ask.

"She isn't my queen," he says through gritted

teeth. I don't understand, but I also don't care why she isn't his queen when he is clearly here to do her bidding. Maybe he just doesn't like the fact that a woman is above him. The older the vampire, the harder it seems to be for them.

"What was it you said you would do to me again?" my sister asks, stepping toward him. She passes by me without even glancing my way.

The vampire leans forward, his hands tied to his sides by my power. "I'll drain you, bitch, mark my words... I *will* drain you."

"You know, my mother once whispered to me an old spell. She had never used it, but her mother before her had heard it worked for her mother." I have absolutely no idea what Tatiana is talking about, but she drops to the ground, her hands digging into the earth as she looks up at the vampire. "I'm going to try it on you," she says with a growing smile.

"Do your worst, bitch. But by the end, you will be under me, in all ways." He cackles, and I shiver at the sound of his laughter.

"To this day, I take from you what you would steal from me.
To this day, I remove from you what you chose to remove from me.

To this day, I borrow from you what you never would have given me."

Her head lifts and she pulls her hands from the dirt, walks toward him, and places her hands on his face as she leans in and kisses his lips. John snarls but does nothing to stop her. The vampire tries to bite her, but I pull his restraints a little tighter, locking his entire body down, including his mouth, as my sister breathes something into him. She steps back on wobbly legs, just as John reaches for her, and she turns to look at me.

"You can free him now."

"What?" I ask, clearly confused.

"Free him. He will do you no harm."

I trust her, even if I did just see her kiss a vampire. So, I do as she says, and the minute I feel the magic creep back into me, the vampire shakes it off and looks to all of us, then his eyes land on Tatiana. "What is it you would have me do?" he asks her, no hostility left in his voice.

"Help the wounded."

"My blood will heal them faster."

My eyes widen at his words. "What?"

"My blood. It heals. All vampires' blood does. We

just chose never to share that fact." He shares the information as if Tatiana were his queen, his sire.

"Heal them, then."

He nods and moves to the first wounded and bites his wrist, offering his blood. They step back, not wanting to take it.

"I gave him a little bit of his soul back," Tatiana states.

"I trust you," John says to Tatiana as he walks over to the vampire. He clearly wants to tear him to shreds, but he takes a small sip of his blood instead, and everyone sucks in a breath and holds it as we wait.

What will it do to him?

Kill him?

Turn him?

That's a whole lot of faith to put into someone you don't fully know.

I get she's his mate, but in reality, they haven't had time to get to know each other. There has been no time for long talks and dates with everything that has been happening.

John pulls back and we all manage to breathe again. It appears nothing bad is happening to him from the blood he drank. He lifts the bloody leg of his jeans, and we watch as the gash that was wide open, closes right before our eyes.

How has no one ever discovered this?

Why is it such a secret?

The lives the vampires could have saved.

The wars this could have ended.

It does nothing but make me angrier.

When John nods his head, the vampire tries again to offer his blood to an injured wolf, and this time they take it, and we all watch as they heal.

When the vampire finally gets to Patrick, he refuses. "No," is all he says before he turns and walks away. I run to catch up to him.

"I'll be fine, Talia. You can go back now."

"I took a lot. I didn't mean to," I say, my voice tight. "Please don't do that again," I whisper.

Patrick turns to look at me. His eyes, which are usually hopeful, are sad, and his mouth sits in a thin line, and I wonder is he in pain, or is it me?

"If you need it, I will do it again," he says, nodding his head and turning away. His upper body is bare from shifting, and I can see all the hard edges and the scars that mar his back. It doesn't lessen his attractiveness—it only improves the way he looks.

"Patrick," I say his name, and he turns back to me.

"I get it. I see it with two clear eyes, Talia. You aren't the same as us mere mortals. You were born to be more, do more."

"I am the same," I say in a voice that whispers lies.

"You aren't. But there is nothing wrong with that

either. You have to stop apologizing and do what you are meant to do. Kick ass."

"Will you let me try to heal you?" It's not something I have ever done on anyone other than Tatiana and Tanya because it does slow me. A lot.

"I'll be fine."

"It was me who drained you. Please, let me." I offer him my hand and he glances at it with his deep brown eyes before he makes a move to step closer and places his warm hand in mine. I suck in a breath and close my eyes as I hold on tight.

"It won't hurt."

"It didn't hurt last time."

"What did it feel like, when I took?"

"Like I was coming down from a high and I needed to close my eyes. That I had no choice but to close them."

His words both shock and amuse me. Tatiana never really explained it to me. I always assumed I knocked them out and that was it.

"I hope this time I don't knock you out." I smirk and close my eyes as I start a small chant and feel the slither of power as it reaches his. It dances with it, healing it as it goes.

"You're smiling. Tell me why," Patrick whispers.

"It's like dancing with your gift. It's magical."

"Talia."

Patrick pulls his hands free and breaks the connection as my sister reaches us. She looks at my glassy eyes, before she turns to Patrick. "Don't let her do that again." Tatiana's hands start touching me to make sure I'm still awake.

"She offered. She said it was painless," Patrick defends.

"It is, but it also knocks her out for days if she does it too much. It drains her."

"Fuck, she didn't tell me that."

"Of course, she didn't," Tatiana says, then looks to John. "Please carry her."

"I can," Patrick says, and before she can say no, I'm swooped up into Patrick's arms and smothered in his warmness before I fall fast asleep.

"**H**ow long is she going to be asleep for?" I hear the complaints, but I can do nothing, my eyes still too heavy.

"**S**he needs to wake. If she doesn't, she may as well be dead." I hear a grunt and then nothing more as sleep takes me once again. I dream of him... I dream of Death. What a silly thing to dream of. But did I expect anything less than dreaming of him?

* * *

This time, I pull myself awake, and when I do, someone is standing above me, her blue eyes smiling as they stare at me.

"You're awake."

I go to move, but I can't. My hands are tied to the ground and so are my feet. Screaming is not an option, as something is swiftly shoved in my mouth. My heart starts to beat so fast in my chest that I feel it vibrate all through me.

I can't move, and *she* has me.

Where is my sister?

Where are Patrick and John?

Oh god, what did I do?

"I expected more of a fight, to be honest. I was prepared. Brought out all my big guns and everything." She bites her cherry-red lips and showcases her bright white teeth. Her gown is silver and large, her boobs basically hanging over the top of it, and I'm afraid if she leans any farther down they will, in fact, fall out.

Turning away from her, my eyes search for a possibility to get out, but there is none. When I look to the door, I see Bronik standing there watching us. Her eyes follow the direction of my glare and she sits next to me.

"So, I heard about your friend." My eyes leave Bronik to find the queen observing me. "How he saves you. And we cannot have that now, can we? So, I created this room. With the help of a few angels, of course." She smiles and it's evil—all the way to the bones evil. "You see, no angel can enter, not even the grim reaper himself."

She licks her teeth, then stretches out next to me and turns her powdered face to stare directly into my eyes. "I will take what you have, as I have always done, and continue to rule. The more you fight, the more it will hurt you." I can't respond because I am still gagged, so she reaches up and removes the cloth, smiling. "Speak."

"Why are you so evil?" I ask. "Did your parents torture you?" I know they didn't. Tatiana told me her parents were amazing.

"No, some of us are just born hungrier than others. I will do anything to maintain my power, and that is something only the great queens know how to do." Her blue eyes stare at mine, unblinking, and I want her to reach out and touch me so I can suck all the power from her body to make her helpless. So she has no choice but to surrender.

"I can see the fight in your eyes, taste it... almost."

She licks her lips. "But you see, those who want it more will succeed. It's how the world works." She goes to touch my dark hair, which has fallen on my face, but she holds off, her hand inches from me. My mind is screaming at her to touch me, just the slightest contact.

A single touch is all I need.

But she doesn't.

She simply smiles.

"I've also heard about your ability, and I want it. So badly. It's the only reason you aren't already dead. You will stay alive until I can work out how I can take it from you. What a power to behold, to be able to steal someone else's power." Her eyes shine with glee as she stares down at me. What she doesn't realize is that I only borrow it, but I don't want her to know any of that. Giving her any more information than she already has won't turn out well for me and even for her.

"Where is my sister?" I ask.

Her eyes glance away, and she looks up to the plain white ceiling above us.

"I almost killed her, but then..." she looks back to me and continues, "...I thought perhaps she could be useful." I watch helplessly as she stands. She puffs her long, silver dress and smiles wickedly. "Don't go anywhere now." She strides over to Bronik, her hand going to his chest as she looks back over her shoulder at me. "He is quite attractive. I had a feeling you would listen to him. Most women do. They can't resist his charms." Her lips lean in and she kisses his cheek, sliding them over until she reaches the edge of his mouth, then bites the corner of his lip. "Delicious, really. I've had a taste and I am willing to share. For a price, of course." I hear her cackle before the clack of her heels takes her away from me.

Hopefully far, far away.

Chapter Twenty-Three

I need to use the bathroom—that's my first thought. My stomach is in so much pain, I'm afraid it's going to burst from the pressure. It's been hours. Hell, it could have been a day since *she* was in here last. There isn't a window to show me what time of day it is, so I have no idea whether the sun has risen or fallen.

I hear footsteps, but no one comes in. I still don't even know how I got here. My eyes were so heavy that it was hard to wake. And I don't know if my sisters are okay. Patrick, John, and the other wolves either. A shiver runs through me as I begin to panic. No one can save me from this. The only person who can help me is me. And I'm afraid I am not strong enough.

I'm broken.

Helpless.

Maybe the prophecy meant someone else.

All this power shouldn't be mine.

If I could give it away, I would.

Tatiana deserves it, she is the stronger sister. Being the oldest and the leader of our family, she should have it all.

Why me? The youngest child born to an earth witch, I don't understand.

My stomach makes a loud noise and I know it's from hunger, but that isn't my main concern. My concern is my bladder. It's so full, I'm think I might soil myself.

The door creaks, drawing my attention, then the queen with her cherry-red lips, as bright as her white teeth shine, enters with a sinister smile aimed right at me.

"I need to use the bathroom."

She laughs, then raises an eyebrow.

The instant relief is like an orgasm I've been holding and keeping at bay. The warmth runs down my legs and I smile at the feeling of my stomach no longer hurting.

"See? Trash." I glance over to see who she's talking to and see Bronik standing next to her. His eyes shine on me, silver and vibrant, as they run the length of my body before looking back to the queen. She lifts a long, ruby-red nail and drags it across his cheek. "Whatever did you see in her anyway?"

He doesn't answer. Instead, he looks away from me and stares at her. I see the way she is looking at him—it's the way I look at Grim.

Something you want but you cannot have.

"I'm going to come back soon and bring a visitor. Aren't you excited to have your first visitor?" the queen asks me.

I say nothing. I don't trust her, and speaking would only spur her on. Plus, I'm currently lying in a puddle of my urine. She doesn't care about me. She cares about only one thing—and that's power.

People in power always win.

I heard that once, and I hope to God it's not true.

I'm getting cold. It's as if the air has become frigid since I woke up. My teeth are chattering from the shivering. The door creaks open again and I turn toward it. What else am I to do, stay where I am doing nothing? I've done enough of that.

Now, I'm getting angry, on top of being hungry and scared.

I want to see my sisters.

I can feel my power simmering below the surface, unable to come out but wanting to more than anything.

"A visitor, as I promised. Bronik is going to sit you in a chair. Remember, Talia, hands to yourself." Bronik carries a chair over and places it behind me, breaks the hold on my wrists, and sits me in it. He grabs each hand and ties them behind my back before he walks back to the door. My feet are still tied, keeping me from being able to make a run for it. I look up again, unable to move, but glad for the change in position.

"Tanya." The word echoes as it leaves my mouth. Tanya stands next to the queen, her head down, biting her lip. My eyes scan over her to make sure she is okay, and I see nothing wrong with her, not even a scratch. In fact, she is dressed well, her hair is done nicely, and her face is glowing. Even if she is hiding half of it from me.

"I see you are happy with your visitor."

I say nothing. It could be an illusion for all I know. But my sister looks alive and well—better than well, actually.

She looks happy.

Apart from right now, where her head is down, and she won't even spare a glance my way.

"Tanya was kind enough to tell us all about you,"

the queen says, and my eyes fall to the queen, looking as happy as a schoolgirl on her first day, as she speaks. I want to tear her words from her throat and shove them back to make her choke on them. But that's impossible in my current state, tied down and covered in urine.

To cut her and watch her bleed would be incredibly satisfying right now.

"You are glad to see your sister, are you not, Tanya? I know you have enjoyed your time here. Would you like to go back and be with your sisters?"

That gets Tanya's attention, and she raises her head to the queen and shakes it, words spluttering from her mouth. "No. No, please, can I stay? I did as you asked."

Tatiana would be so sad right now to witness this.

Me? Well, it simply makes me angry. Furious. Tanya has a good heart, and the queen has been using that to her advantage.

"Of course you can. Just tell your sister to give me what is mine, and you can stay here with me."

I glare at the queen, her mouth a thin line as she glares back.

"I know you have to give it, I'm not stupid."

The problem is, she is stupid. This power that I have isn't mine to give. I take, borrow, but I cannot give power.

I hold my head high as I look directly into her eyes. "You must be, because if you were smart, you would know I cannot give it."

She moves, and in an instant, she is standing in front of me. She is careful not to touch me as she leans in close. So close I can smell the mint on her breath.

"If you can take, you can always give. It only means we have to work out how. And believe me, trash, we will find a way for me to have what you have. Even if I have to make a deal with the devil. I've done it before, and I will do it again."

Ignoring the queen, I see my sister staring at me. She looks down to the floor when my eyes meet hers.

"Tanya, Tatiana is waiting for you to come home." Tanya's eyes close and she squeezes them tight.

The queen steps back until she is next to her and places a hand on her arm. "But she is home, aren't you, my dear?"

Tanya nods her head, not disagreeing with her.

Then the queen addresses me again, "But I do have someone else I thought I would maybe bring in to persuade you. I was hoping you would do so easily, knowing how I have looked after your sister so well. But you haven't, so I guess we'll have to try another way." Her hands raise and she claps them once.

Bronik walks in, grabs hold of Tanya, and steps her

back, keeping his hand in hers as another angel steps into the room this time. He is carrying someone over his shoulder, and when I see who it is, I try to move against the ropes tying me down, but I can't move. It's impossible.

"Seems he is a good tracker, tracked you to me all by himself." Queen Veronica walks over and touches Patrick's hair, lifting it as he lies over the angel's shoulder, passed out.

"Let him go. He has nothing to do with any of it." My voice is broken, and it cracks, having not used it much.

"Lies. All the wolves will be dead soon. Thinking they can side with you is not a possibility. They will pay for their disobedience with their lives." She spits the words like venom from her lips. "Lay him down, then we shall play." Queen Veronica looks back to Tanya. "You can stay." Tanya nods like a well-trained puppy, and I keep the tears at bay that she is choosing this life over us.

It hurts.

It hurts so fucking much.

"I like to play with my subjects. I was going to be nice to your family. To only get rid of you and let them live their lives normally. But then you had to go and do that disappearing act of yours. I wonder why it is that Death saves you."

I have no answer for her because I don't know why he chooses to save me. It's a mystery to us both.

"No matter, though. He can't reach us in here, so he will never know what pain you are about to endure." Patrick is placed in a chair and bound to it the same way I am, but he has extra rope around his hands.

"Patrick..." I say his name, but he doesn't move. I lean over as far as I can go to hear if he is still breathing. When I hear a slight release of breath, a sigh of relief rushes over me.

She hasn't killed him.

Yet.

"Patrick is under a spell," the queen says, then reaches her hand out and touches his head, waking him. He moves his head slightly before a loud roar rips from him as he tries to move. It's useless, though. Neither of us can move and we are both tied down, unable to do anything. "Now." She claps her hands. "He is awake."

I don't spare her a glance. Instead, I keep my eyes trained on Patrick. His deep brown eyes lock on me, searching me over to make sure I am okay, before he turns his nose up.

He can smell it.

Shit.

His eyes fall to my pants, and he growls.

"Oh, hush, puppy. It's you, you should be worried

about, not this precious bird over here." She nods her head, and a vampire walks in through the door. I watch helplessly as he strides over to Patrick and then tears his shirt off him. Patrick doesn't even flinch at the action. The vampire leans down, and I watch as his fangs protrude until they touch Patrick's skin and he bites, taking something precious that isn't his. Patrick remains still throughout, and my heart hurts for him, breaks for him.

"Why?" I question as I watch the color leave Patrick's face.

"We can't have him at his full strength now, can we? This is the fastest way to drain him, and it's quite efficient if you ask me." I can hear the smile in her voice, so I don't have to look at her face to know it's there.

Bitch.

The vampire pulls away and Patrick's head bobs before he manages to steady himself and lock eyes with me again. Two puncture marks now mar his neck, joining with his other scars, but he doesn't seem to care.

"Patrick, Patrick, Patrick... why would you choose to follow such a lowly being when you could have chosen to follow the queen?" she asks him.

"Because you are evil, worse than any other human, as bad as the shit under my boot, and do not deserve the position of power you have. You steal, break shit, hurt people to get where you are. A true queen would never do that to her people," Patrick says proudly, all the while keeping his eyes locked on mine.

"How wrong you are. A true queen will do whatever is necessary to get to where she wants to be. You really think your precious Talia here could kill someone close to her if it meant saving others? No, she couldn't. I can tell you that much. But if you don't believe me, ask her sister." The queen waves Tanya forward.

She takes a few steps, looks up with her emerald eyes and answers, "You couldn't. We both know it, Sister." Then she steps back and looks back to the floor. As if she isn't betraying me with every word. Every step. Not just me, but our entire family and Tatiana who has loved us more than life itself.

"See? Now, wolf, are you sure you want to stay on that side?"

Patrick doesn't answer, but we all know what his answer is, as he holds his head up high and locks his eyes with mine.

"Have it your way, then." The queen grasps his shoulder, then smiles. "Now remember, Talia, we can stop this anytime you want. You just have to give me your power."

"Don't you dare. You let me die... do not give her

anything," Patrick says to me as her nails dig into his skin.

"As you wish, wolf." She smiles as her nails start to draw blood and it trickles down his skin.

Chapter Twenty-Four

Patrick is screaming, and I am helpless to stop it.

She hasn't stopped.

First, she bled him with her nails. Dragging them all over his chest, carving her name into his skin, telling him when he is buried it's her name they will remember, not his.

Now she is tearing his nails from his nail beds. Three have gone as she smiles, lifting them with her magic and pulling them free.

I have to look away, I can't stand to watch this disaster play out even a second longer.

"Look, trash, look."

I ignore her words, but cold hands pull my head back to face Patrick who is still strapped to his seat in front of me.